A-1 Bookstore
6067 Navarre Rd., SW. 44706
(330) 477-0908
New-Used-Paperback-Hard

They were better than forty days out from the Uranus shell, when something happened which was so inexplicable that had they not seen it for themselves they would never have believed it. The instruments remained silent, but those sensitive to light warned suddenly of something strange in the region of perfect darkness into which they were heading. Ancor leaped into his scanners immediately, but it was only in the visual spectrum that a picture came.

Out in the midst of the great wastes of Nepturanspace there hung a huge and solitary eye.

D1571080

CAGEWORLD SERIES

by Colin Kapp

THE
TYRANT
OF HADES

Cageworld 3

Colin Kapp

DAW BOOKS, INC.
DONALD A. WOLLHEIM, PUBLISHER

1633 Broadway, New York, NY 10019

Copyright ©, 1982, by Colin Kapp.

A DAW Book by arrangement with New English Library.

All Rights Reserved.

Cover art by Vincent Di Fate.

First DAW Printing, March 1984

1 2 3 4 5 6 7 8 9

DAW TRADEMARK REGISTERED
U.S. PAT. OFF. MARCA
REGISTRADA. HECHO EN U.S.A.

PRINTED IN U.S.A.

CHAPTER ONE

Mystery on the Liss-Mal

ZAPOKETA ON THE Saturn Shell. Across the worn and tattered lawns of Nexon Square old Imref Varter came, prying into trash cans, pocketing an occasional piece of metal in the bag-like folds of his voluminous and shabby coat, and generally appearing as disreputable as the seedy square across which he moved. Casual observation would have placed him well over sixty years of age, and his hair was a shorn, stiff stubble which blended so completely with his beard that his head was a virtual ball of fur from which protruded two eyes surmounting ruddy cheeks, a nose, and the occasional flash of surprisingly red lips. One leg was seriously twisted, and this gave his movements an odd, rolling effect, as though he lived on his own private sea, yet for all this his frame was fully erect, and his eyes were constantly alive and watchful in a way that stamped him as no ordinary down and out morsel of humanity.

Despite his generally formidable appearance, the children playing in the square paid him no attention. For many months now his ragged eccentricity had been recognised and accepted in the district. He was regarded as a character to be ignored rather than shunned or feared, and so little impact did his comings and goings now evoke that few could truthfully have remembered where they last saw Imref, and if so, when. This situation of 'non presence' suited him nicely. He wanted and needed no confidants, and it kept him below the threshold level of notice by the police. He had a job to do for which invisibility would have suited him even better, but lacking the invention of so vital a cloak, he made clever use of its psychological equivalent: whatever he did or wherever he went, nobody wanted to know.

One far edge of Nexon Square gave suddenly on to the Liss-mal, a street of many characters, and one of the most

5

important thoroughfares of the Zapoketa conurbation. Here a mixture of theatres and clubs and places of entertainment vied with shops and restaurants for the rich pickings from those who regarded the Liss-mal as the hub of the universe. Somewhere in this hotch-potch of commercial developments, where land values were so high that had diamonds been discovered in the earth it would not have paid to dig them out, one could find an establishment to cater for virtually every conceivable need and taste, and one could never be surprised at how bizarre or how mundane these wants could be. Thus next to the "sex palace" of Mistress Sin, probably one of the most expensive and exclusive brothels ever devised, came something called "*Cherry's Amazing Holo-Theatre*" currently showing a three-dimensional hologram presentation called A FANTASY JOURNEY THROUGH THE UNIVERSE OF SOLARIA. This in turn was adjacent to a single door which bore the simple message: MAQ ANCOR. REGISTERED ASSASSIN.

It was indeed in these three particular establishments that Imref Varter was interested. They were all housed under the same roof in a purpose-designed building in one of the more expensive sections of the Liss-mal, and his painstaking research had shown that, building costs and land values taken into consideration, not one of these enterprises could be considered a viable commercial proposition. Admittedly the "palace" of Mistress Sin was deservedly popular, but she could have operated the same sort of establishment in the better-class "red-light" district for only one hundredth part of her current rent. True also that *Cherry's Amazing Holo-Theatre* was playing to full capacity, but his admission prices were so low that Imref, after keeping a careful tally, knew that Cherry was scarcely covering his daily operating costs. And as for Ancor the Assassin—in three months the man had received not one single client, for the simple reason that those with assassination on their minds had better sense than to walk boldly in through a blatantly-marked door on the most public thoroughfare in Zapoketa.

As his intelligence briefing had suggested, these three establishments had to be a front for something else, but despite many months of patient surveillance and enquiry, Imref Varter found himself still no nearer knowing what shadowy organisation lurked behind these intriguing exteriors. The proprietors seldom left their establishments, the telephone and video taps had picked up nothing at all suspicious, and his own watch for visits by subversive agents had been a complete waste of time. Left to make his own decisions, Imref would have written the case off as an innocuous mystery. Unfortunately his superior in the Service,

6

Dil Carras, was not as easily convinced. There was the question of the great bonded sky-carriers which occasionally made deliveries to the rooftop wharf, usually after dark.

Working his way into the Liss-mal, Imref passed in front of the discreetly curtained "palace" of Mistress Sin. One of the windows had been opened, and the curtains were blowing wide in the breeze. Pausing in his vagrant way, Imref looked in. Several of the local girls who worked in the "palace" were joking with an outstandingly attractive girl with a remarkably greenish skin-tone, who he knew to be the legendary Mistress Sin herself. Although he had had the Saturn Identifile carefully researched, he had been unable to discover her real identity—but this was not too surprising, because the Identifile list for the whole shell contained nearly five times ten to the twenty-second power of names. This number was so unthinkable that had it been possible to review ten names every second, scanning through the entire list would have taken around one and a half million million centuries. Of course, looking only at the female side of the file should have taken only half that time.

The laughing green girl saw the curtains blowing and came over to fix them, noticed Imref outside the window, and threw him out a handful of coins, which he pocketed with every sign of gratitude. The gift of money was a handsome sum but insignificant when compared to his salary as a top-level intelligence agent; but the incident gave him the opportunity of examining this green-skinned enigma from a close distance. He found the experience unexpectedly heady and delicious. She was a natural coquette, and an artist as well, but for all her charms the keen and calculating intelligence which nestled in her eyes was not lost on him, and he made a mental note that she must never be underestimated.

Imref Varter passed on then across the front of *Cherry's Amazing Holo-Theatre*, slightly dazzled by the moving three-dimensional images in the showcases, which purported to be scenes from the concentric inner shells which lay within the Saturn shell itself. The power and artistry of such images was immediate and obvious, and Imref felt it difficult to relate such genius to the wizened and bearded little man in sandals and white toga who was fussing around the installation of a new display. He knew this to be Cherry, the owner of the show, and Imref would have mentally marked him as a fool, except that no fool could possibly have produced a holo-show so advanced in technique and so imaginative in form and content. Again, here was one of whom it was wise to be wary.

Imref's third stop was actually against the door marked: MAQ ANCOR. REGISTERED ASSASSIN.

. That Ancor was a registered assassin was probably beyond dispute, but the league or guild with which he was registered had not yet been located. Under cover of a pretended paroxysm of coughing, Imref leant against the wall and tested the door. As always, it was locked, and the slight strip of adhesive tape which he had placed there several days before showed that the entrance could not have been used in the intervening period. He had only twice seen Ancor himself, and what he had seen had been impressive: the man looked like a lion and walked like a cat, had proved impossible to shadow without certain risk of detection, and kept trained fingers perpetually within inches of the weapon pouches at his hips. Of all the mysterious trio on the Liss-mal, Varter had decided, Maq Ancor was undoubtedly the most dangerous.

Continuing on his way along the crowded pavements of the Liss-mal, Imref then took a circuitous route through the side streets which fetched him finally back to the vicinity of Nexon Square. Here, in an alley between the delivery bays of two large stores, was located a public video-phone booth. Entering, he spoke a number carefully into the voice-responsive call mechanism, and when the indicator told him that contact had been established, he felt for the concealed button which would scramble the call beyond all possibility of unauthorised interception. The screen remained dark.

"Dil?"

"Listening, Imref. What's new?"

"Nothing's new. The last piece of action was that sky-carrier consignment three days ago."

"We tried to check on that. But it was a bonded transit container which had been through so many carriers' hands and had its documentation changed so many times that it was impossible to say what was supposed to be in it or where it came from."

"I still think we're chasing rainbows, Dil," said Varter. "There's not the slightest suggestion of anything illegal or subversive down on that part of the Liss-mal—which is a heap more than I can say for some of the areas adjacent. Why don't we stop wasting time on this one, and let me get back to doing something where we get some results to show for the effort?"

"I still can't agree with you, Imref. I've a gut feeling about that place. We've managed to get hold of the architect's plans of the building, and do you know there's a workshop at the back of it so large you could build a battlecruiser in there?"

"So what? Anyone mad enough to try to produce holo-scenes of the whole Solarian universe needs a big workshop. I've seen the show, and the effects are shattering. The wonder to me is

8

that such trick holo-shots could be produced in so small a space."

"Well I'm not convinced. But I agree with you that it's high time we moved on to other things. So I propose to have one last crack at busting this thing open."

"How do you intend to do that, Dil?"

"I've sat behind this damn desk too long. I want to get back into the field again for a bit. I'm coming down to Zapoketa, and you and I are going to penetrate right into that place and discover what really does go on."

Imref Varter was silent for a moment, then: "I can't advise it, Dil. I know you spent many years in the field, but you never were a big-city boy."

"What are you saying?"

"I'm saying Zapoketa's the type of place that you were either born into or else you don't bother with. I couldn't trust you to get from the Terminal to the Liss-mal with all your luggage intact and without you being mugged on the way. If you want a penetration made, I'll do it on my own. Frankly, I think you'd just be a liability."

"That's the trouble with you field men. You always get to thinking that anyone who sits behind a desk automatically becomes deaf, blind, and daft. Well, I've got news for you, Imref. I'm still a better field man than you'll ever be—which is why I head the department while you're still out there gathering moss. I'll be at the Zapoketa Terminal in two days. Meet me there, and have your plans prepared. I'm giving myself twenty-four hours to crack something the rest of you haven't been able to solve in nine months. How does that sound for an executive decision?"

"Have it your way, Dil," said Imref. "But let the records show I was against your coming. If this thing does blow up in our faces I'd like at least a little something going for me."

Although Imref's tone was light, his face was undoubtedly grave as he cut the connection and turned away. Something about the strange mystery on the Liss-mal made him feel certain that what Dil Carras was proposing to do was unquestionably foolhardy. The look he had seen in the eyes of Mistress Sin, and Maq Ancor's catlike tread, convinced him that whatever it was in that building was no ordinary thing. He and Dil would have to tread warily indeed if they planned an unauthorised entry.

CHAPTER TWO

Alien Dream

THE TOWNSHIP OF Bryhn on the Mars shell, in the principality of Hammanite. A small patch of light in the gloom of an underground room. In the centre, under the light, a low post of no apparent significance, and atop the post the golden spines of a thousand-way multiple-circuit electrical connector. And a drama . . .

The air in the low cell was so hot as to be almost unbreathable, yet it was tension not temperature which caused the respiration of its occupant to become painful and slow. Confined in a wheeled tank containing his life-support systems and from which only his arms and the top of his torso protruded, Prince Awa-Ce-Land-a felt the warm air sear his straining lungs and watched the monitors below his chin light one after the other with a warning of the imminence of death. Centrally in his thoughts was the dreadful terminal connection under the single lamp. If he had strength and equanimity, he could ignore it, and somehow or the other, with his life-support mechanisms racing out of synchronisation, he would die. He feared however, that as before, when the great monster of permanent extinction seriously challenged his psyche, his resolve would crumble. He would propel himself towards the post, and, taking his own wired connector in his hand, he would once more make that fearful hook-up.

If he did so, then he knew he would survive. His artificial body-processes, again re-sequenced by the most powerful computer in the Solarian universe, would respond immediately and give him great ease and a renewed interest in living. He would be transported from the virtual edge of death and given a literal new lease of life. It was a situation greatly to be desired, and he had done it many times before, but after the first time what had always tempted him to stay his hand was not the process of physical rejuvenation but the accompanying . . .

10

ALIEN DREAMS!!!

Whilst that frightful connector was in place every aspect of his being and existence was totally coupled to Zeus, the cybernetic complex which was so powerful that it had taken over from man the task of constructing and regulating the entire Solarian universe. But the linkage brought far more than an adjustment to his physical condition. Whilst the connection remained, even his brain shared some staggering empathy with the artificial intelligence of the giant machine. Although he soon became lost in the gulfs and voids between its mammoth electronic concepts, he was forced mentally to reach out and touch that most frightening entity of all . . . artificial intelligence . . . the machine Id . . . the personality which was the great computer itself. And thus locked together, great, alien dreams would flow from a mind never born of flesh and blood into one only too appallingly dependent on continuing blood supply . . . oxygen . . . the removal of waste products . . .

ALIEN DREAMS!!!

The last of the monitors flared red, and Land-a knew he had very few seconds left in which to reach a decision. Already there was a whistling in his ears rising steadily in intensity, and only his own weak chest muscles were forcing the shallowed movements of his rib cage in the tank. The light before his eyes suddenly seemed intolerably bright, whilst the relative gloom became a sea of impenetrable darkness, and the great shadows of permanent death appeared to hover over his head like dark angels. He looked at the hand which held the fateful coupling, and was frightened by the way it was ghastly white and shaking. Then he made his final deliberate choice, and the coupling dropped down out of sight. He had decided to die rather than once more face the . . .

ALIEN DREAMS!!!

Then panic hit him like the explosion of a bomb. He had already left it nearly too late for recovery, but the mentally-controlled mechanics of the propulsion system on his tank responded even where muscles might have failed. Hauling the connector back and slamming the self-aligning surfaces on to the terminal plate was quite literally performed with the last remnants of his swiftly-failing energy, and Land-a actually fainted as the connection was made.

He was plunged into ALIEN DREAMS, and these were dreams

such as never played in any human brain. The universe was set beneath him, as though he were God, but there was nothing god-like about the interpretation of the scene. Instead, there was an unearthly dispassion and a sense of objectivity, a comprehension of detail which analysed every fragment of every scene down to the most microscopic detail yet simultaneously still encompassed the whole. And strange were the alien fantasies which rode the scene, touched with a curious sense of searching and longing, as though the machine which had built the Solarian universe was looking for something greater than itself with which to share and confirm its sense of being.

Then came the black dreams, the haunting insecurities, the weaknesses and the fears. Like any other advanced intelligence, this vast intellect was riddled with self-doubt and worries about the things it was unable to overcome, and it was in the midst of this traumatic self-search that Land-a saw the tyrant of Hades. Admittedly the view was through a vastly alien perception, but nonetheless it was recognisable as a very potent reality.

The wheeled man had no way of knowing how long these fantasies continued. When he awoke finally, feeling refreshed and renewed, he remained motionless for a long time, stupefied by the imagery which had been impressed into his brain, and trying to shake the trail of alien impressions from his head. Then he drew himself together, wheeled rapidly from the room, and headed for the nearest communications point. Stabbing at the buttons with fingers now cool and precise, he raised his own control operator.

"Get me the Centre for Solarian Studies at Ajkavit. I want to get a message to Maq Ancor."

From his observation point high in the building, Maq Ancor had watched Imref's perambulation along the Liss-mal with a thoughtful frown. Soon the micro-transmitter built into one of the coins which Sine Anura had thrown to the agent became activated by the warmth of the fellow's pocket and enabled Maq to track his progress back on a way parallel to that by which he had come, and finally to be able to record the conversation in the videophone booth. The exercise told him nothing new about Imref Varter, whose interest had always been obvious to one with an assassin's trained instincts. The new piece of information was of the intended penetration of their premises, and it was this that brought deep lines of speculation into the multiple folds of Ancor's complex face.

He picked up the internal communicator.

"Nice work, Sine! That bugged coin worked beautifully! But the natives are more restless than we thought."

"I wish we didn't have to do it this way, Maq—in secret. Surely the authorities on Mars shell could have made some sort of contact with the Saturn shell authorities and arranged for us to have a base here legitimately?"

"You know their reasoning, Sine. A lot of the population on the Saturn shell are direct descendants of enforced emigrants from the Mars shell. Let it be known that there is a route through the shells other than the emigrant route via the spoke shuttles, and all hell could break loose."

"Then how much longer before we continue on our way? If they're watching us that closely, it won't be long before they start taking action."

"They're already planning it. Somebody called Dil is coming to Zapoketa in a couple of days to join up with our fuzzy old friend Imref. They intend breaking in here to see what we're up to. The *Shellback*'s quite ready to fly, but we've the final consignment of stores arriving by sky-carrier in three days' time. It will take us a couple of days to unload the transit container and stow the stuff away, so we can't reasonably leave here inside a week. But I think we must expect visitors before then."

"Maq, how could they get in? Not even a mouse could get through all that steel and concrete."

"I don't know how they'll try it, but I've developed a healthy respect for old Imref. Obvious he may be, but he knows just when to come and when to fade, and he's sharp with it. If Imref reckons he can penetrate here, then he probably can."

"So how will we play it, Maq?"

"It depends on the way they start the game. If they come in shooting, we don't have much option but to kill them. But if they make a reasonable approach, I think between us we've enough talents to keep them occupied."

"Any further word from Professor Soo at Ajkavit?"

"Not yet, but they're seven hundred and forty-four million miles distant, so the message journey time is around an hour each way." He glanced up as an indicator lit on the screen. "Ah! There's something coming in now. I'll get it decoded and let you know."

AJKAVIT UNIVERSITY: SOO CALLING ANCOR. YOUR SUSPICIONS CONFIRMED. LAND-A NOW ADMITS HE DOES ENTER A FORM OF EMPATHIC COUPLING WITH ZEUS WHILE HIS LIFE-SUPPORT SYSTEMS ARE BEING TUNED. THE EMPATHY MANIFESTS ITSELF AS A FORM OF DREAM STATE OR DELIRIUM RATHER THAN A

DIALOGUE, AND APPEARS TO BE A WINDOW INTO ZEUS'
DEEPER THOUGHT PROCESSES RATHER THAN A DELIB-
ERATE ATTEMPT BY THE COMPUTER TO CONTROL OR
COMMUNICATE WITH THE MAN. YOUR PLANNED EXPE-
DITION INTO HADES-SPACE SEEMS TO HAVE ITS ORI-
GIN IN ONE OF THESE EMPATHIC ENCOUNTERS, AND
THE SAME ENCOUNTER MAY BE WHAT PROMPTED
LAND-A TO ASK THE QUESTION "WHAT REALLY DOES
HAPPEN TO THE ENFORCED EMIGRANTS WHO ARE CAR-
RIED BY THE SPOKEWAYS BEYOND THE SHELL OF
SATURN".

Ancor transmitted a copy of this to both Cherry and Sine,
checked that all his security arrangements were fully operational,
then went back to the workshop which housed the *Shellback*
while it was being prepared for their latest expedition through the
universe of Solaria. Although he had seen it a thousand times
before, he never ceased to be amazed at the supreme ugliness of
the little ship, which traded all the niceties of conventional
aero-space design for the sheer brute strength of its multiple
engines and virtually inexhaustible sources of power. In the
confines of the workshop the blocked squareness of the little
craft, complex with weapon and instrument projections, made an
even greater than usual impact, screaming of strength and utility
and the toughness of its shields and the power of its armaments.
Although remarkably scarred by sundry forms of violence on
previous expeditions, its hull was still as sound as a bell, and
Ancor patted it affectionately as he climbed into the hatch.

"How's it going, Tez?"

Tez, having done his stint as Cherry's holo-projectionist, was
now engaged in the intricate task of checking and packing the
stores they would need in the months ahead.

Tez scratched his head. "Nearly finished with this lot, Maq.
Then we've one further load to come, and we're ready for
take-off. But it beats me how the *Shellback* ever manages to
stagger into the air under the weight of all this lot."

"It's done on the principle of sheer brute force applied at just
the right angle. Did you know those new motors Land-a had
fitted must be around the most powerful that have ever been
devised. If we run them up to full speed, they're calculated to
give us a space-mode velocity of half a million miles an hour,
which is five times faster than we've ever gone before."

"Why do we need such an incredible speed, Maq?"

"In terms of the distances between the outer shells, the speed
isn't incredible at all. The shell of Uranus is eight hundred and
ninety-seven million miles from here, and even at our new

14

speed it will take us all of seventy-five days to reach it. And from Uranus to the Neptune shell is even farther. So such velocities are an absolute necessity if we're ever to do any form of exploration in a reasonable time.''

"What ever happened to those faster than light drives we used to read about as kids?''

"Unfortunately they remain the fiction they always were. Nobody could get around Einstein's theory of relativity, and nobody ever will. The *Shellback* is by far the fastest thing in space, and even that is nearing the limits of the maximum speed it will ever be theoretically possible to achieve. We don't know what lies outside Solaria, but unless there's something closer than one-hundredth part of a light year, we aren't ever going to be able to reach it. And even that journey would take the *Shellback* thirteen years. That's the reality with the fiction stripped away.''

CHAPTER THREE

Under Attack

THE CONURBATION OF Zapoketa on the Saturn shell had grown up around the Hyper-Travel Terminal, which now stood roughly at its centre. Key to the whole complex was the vast golden tube of the Spokeways system, operated by Zeus, whose shuttles constantly raced to cope with the draft of enforced emigrants who daily arrived at its daunting maw. The emigrants were chosen by a computer-based lottery, in which every person born on the shell was registered in the Saturn Identifile, and before they reached marriageable age would receive one of two decisions: irrevocable permission to stay on the shell, or an unalterable command to report to their nearest Spokeway terminal for emigration to some new and outer shell being opened-up for habitation.

The system was harsh and greatly disliked, but with the shell population doubling roughly every thirty years, there were no practical alternatives: some had to leave in order that those who remained had space to live. Even the staggering five times ten to the eighteenth power square miles of habitable land on the Saturn shell, much of it still underpopulated, could not cope with many successive doublings of the population before reaching saturation and a gradual breakdown of facilities and resources. It was a wry fact that if the Saturn shell ever did reach a full level of population, then in a mere thirty years they would need another shell of equivalent size, and in sixty years, another two!

Thus enforced emigration, as unwelcome as it was, was a painful reality of life, and respect for the principle was a fundamental tenet in the structure of all the diverse modes of society which thrived on the surface of the shell. In order to bring in this unending stream of people from the vast areas served by each of the spokes, the Spokeways terminal inevitably became the centre

16

of a multi-mode travel complex which also engaged in all the other aspects of commercial and passenger transport, and it was on the ready availability of these facilities that the vast conurbations like Zapoketa grew.

Dil Carras would be arriving by exospheric liner after a twenty-four hour flight which would have brought him nearly a million miles from his base in Margram. Although he remained as fuzzy, Imref Varter had exchanged his baggy coat for a neater and less conspicuous soft grey suit, and was now picking his way across the vast terminal concourse towards the exospheric arrival bays. The queues of emigrants waiting for their shuttles depressed him. They were those for whom life had apparently been torn asunder, and they waited pale-faced and nervous or in tears for their turn to step into the fateful vessels which would take them . . . where? They were themselves descended from sometime emigrants from other, inner shells, and logic suggested that this was merely the same pattern being repeated. Unfortunately, the shuttles ran one way only—ever outward through Solaria—and no emigrant had ever been able to return to tell about the place to which he had been transported.

Breaking free of these wan queues, Varter quickened his step, his twisted leg giving him the semblance of a merry, rolling motion as he attempted to reach the gate through which Dil Carras would emerge. Despite having once been a useful man in the field, Dil had never been exposed to the ways of a hypermetropolis such as Zapoketa, and his last few years spent on purely administrative chores would not have improved the situation. His stance and consternation at first encountering such an overwhelming scene would immediately mark him as a stranger, and therefore make him fair game for the amazing range of con-men, pickpockets, muggers, extortionists, and other criminals who made a rich living from the innocents who daily arrived by their millions at the terminal and its environs. Whilst it superficially seemed ridiculous to think of an intelligence agent becoming an easy victim for a petty criminal, it was precisely because Dil would consider himself untouchable that he would fall so easily.

A sudden thickening of the crowd delayed Imref for a while, and by the time he had fought his way through, Dil Carras had some time previously emerged through the arrival gate. From the thunderstruck look on Dil's face, Imref guessed what had happened. Carras had already lost his return ticket for the million mile trip to a bogus uniformed "inspector", and doubtless that same ticket, probably worth a third of Imref's yearly salary, had

17

already been sold to a passenger awaiting a flight at a cheaper stand-by rate. It might be possible to recover the ticket or arrange its cancellation, but in the ensuing fuss there was an even chance that most of Dil's luggage would go missing, and the near certainty that his pockets would be emptied of valuables.

Nearby, an old lady, trapped in the crush, tottered and fell to the ground, Carras started forward to help recover the few pitiful possessions which her dropped bag spilled on the ground. Varter merely growled, threw Carras a couple of security wrist-straps with which to maintain control of his cases, and literally forced his superior away through the crowds to where the hover-taxis slid smoothly down the exit ramp. Snatching at the door of an already-moving taxi, Varter threw himself inside, crushing one of Carras's cases into the seat with him. Dil hesitated, released his remaining cases to the driver, and watched carefully as they were stowed into the vehicle's luggage pod. Then he climbed in alongside Varter, and his face was rueful.

"This is one bloody hell of a place!" he said.

Varter did not answer. He was doing two things simultaneously: watching the road to ensure that the driver made not the slightest deviation from the route he had been instructed to follow, and watching the luggage pod to make sure that nobody removed the luggage during their frequent halts at jams and intersections. Only when they reached the relative security of the room in the third-rate hotel which he had reserved for them did he condescend to become vocal, and then it was mainly to let loose a torrent of swearwords when it was found that the instruments and documents in the cases which had been in the luggage pod had been mysteriously converted into house-bricks during the journey.

"Of all the blind, stupid idiots, Dil," he said finally, "you must be about the shell's greatest. When travelling through Zapoketa, keep all your money in a locked money belt next to your skin, carry only one piece of luggage, and hold on to it at all times no matter how inconvenient or whatever anybody tells you the rules may be. And be particularly on the look-out for kindly old ladies who faint in the crush, or the pretty young thing who hollers because somebody snatched her purse. There's a regular training school for fainting old ladies and purseless maidens, and even if you only stop to watch instead of trying to help, you can certainly lose your luggage and probably the contents of your pockets as well."

Slightly white-faced, Dil Carras was still staring at the bricks which had come to occupy his cases.

18

"My God! My God!" he said. "What a hell of a place! Did you know the bastards even took my tie—and I was wearing it at the time."

"Mmm!" Imref showed no evidence of surprise. "Some of those boys are so clever they could shave the pubic hair off you while you're walking along, and you'd never even notice."

"Don't say you told me so!"

"I wouldn't waste my breath on it, Dil. I've been doing some research on to how we can get into that place on the Liss-mal. The whole building is tighter than a drum, and their intruder-alarm system is set to detect anything from a big flea upwards. I've even seen it triggered by a bumble-bee. And as for the fellow who claims to be an assassin—well, I think it's probably true. He's got eyes in the back of his head and the soles of his feet as well, as far as I can tell. I can't tail him even with a team of five, and he'd be a useful fellow to have around if ever we want to re-write our training manuals, because he knows more tricks than you, I, and the rest of the criminal fraternity of Zapoketa all rolled into one."

"You're not suggesting we call it off, are you, Imref?"

"Not at all. I think I've discovered their Achilles-heel. And if we're going to make that penetration effectively, it's going to have to be done in a very special way. That will take a great deal of string-pulling by somebody like you."

Dil Carras glanced around the seedy room with obvious distaste.

"How can I pull any strings from a place like this?"

Varter pulled a small, shabby, decrepit case out from under the bed, opened it, and showed it to contain a remarkably powerful and comprehensive radio transmitter and receiver. "This will easily put you in touch with Margram Base, and the strings can be pulled from there. Now here's exactly what I suggest we do . . ."

The crash of the intruder alarm woke Ancor instantly from his bed. The succeeding barrage of sounds, however, took him not towards the alarm panel but to the window which looked out over the now-dark Liss-mal. A large heavy-goods vehicle loaded with what appeared to be concrete blocks had come hurtling at speed across Nexon Square and plunged straight through the frontage of Mistress Sin's "palace" taking most of the wall with it. Such was the force of the impact that had the vehicle had a driver, he would certainly be dead, but Ancor suspected that its control would have been entirely automatic, and the whole "accident" quite deliberate. He regarded it as quite a good move

19

on the part of Imref Varter, because in order to still the jangling
bells, Ancor would be forced to put a large segment of his alarm
system out of operation. Varter could not have known, however,
that between Mistress Sin's and the workshop there was a further
bulkhead of solid concrete and steel which it would be difficult to
penetrate even with explosives.

Ancor had switched out of circuit the alarms which still responded to the impact of the crash, and was about to call the
Zapoketa police to come and investigate the damage when the
bells broke out for the second time. This time it was a fire-alert
from the region of his own office at the end of the building, and
he considered it probable that someone had thrown an incendiary
device in through the glass panel of the door. He had no fears
about containing the fire, because the whole area could be
flooded with carbon dioxide from the firecontrol panel, but a
second segment of his alarm system had to be taken out of
operation, and his respect for Imref Varter increased considerably.
Whilst he wondered what Imref's next move would be, he
contacted Sine and Cherry and the others and sent them all to
the workshop. It was only two hours before the sky-carrier was
due to arrive at the rooftop wharf with the final delivery of
stores, so such an assembly was nearly due anyway, and they
would be safer there than elsewhere in the building.

The third set of waking alarms indicated the presence of an
actual intruder in Cherry's holo-theatre. This Ancor viewed as
more serious because, although the bulkhead behind Mistress
Sin's continued also behind the theatre, there were at least two
doors, both firmly locked, which led through to the main part of
the building and the workshop beyond. He knew these doors
would not be easy to open, but having gained some idea of
Varter's resourcefulness, Ancor was not prepared to accept that
they were inviolable. He put through his call to the Zapoketa
police, then went and stationed himself in the corridor from
where he could keep an eye on both doors in case one should be
opened and an entry attempted.

Even as he placed himself and primed his weapons, however,
he sensed that something was amiss. Even despite the two
previous false alarms, Varter must have known that the theatre
would still be monitored, and he would be unlikely to make such
a blatantly obvious attempt at penetration. Was it possible that
this, too, was just another decoy, and that the actual entry was
being made elsewhere? Ancor called Tez down to take his place
and guard the doors, whilst he carried out a rapid inspection of
all the other possible points of entry. Having satisfied himself
that they were all safe and under no form of attack, he was about

to relieve Tez in the corridor when the drone of approaching
motors overhead made him change his mind. The sky-carrier was
approaching the rooftop wharf, and despite the emergency, there
was other work to do.

CHAPTER FOUR

The Deadly Mistress Sin

ABOVE THE ROOFTOP wharf the great sky-carrier was hovering on pillars of fire. Once Ancor had signalled his readiness to receive the consignment, a large central portion of the ship broke away to reveal itself as a transit container, which was carefully lowered on stout steel cables. Tonight's drop was longer than usual, because Ancor had decided against stripping the contents of the container in the wharf, and had retracted the deck of the reception pad with hydraulic rams so that the container could continue its journey right down to the floor of the workshop itself.

Keeping the sky-carrier in exactly the right position while such a long drop was made through such a relatively small aperture was difficult, and it required a lot of talk-back to the sky-carrier's controller to ensure the placement went without a hitch. Whilst he was thus in position on the wharf's observation tower, Ancor could also see the arrival of the Zapoketa police and disaster squads to the front of the building where the crash and the fire had taken place. In addition to the overhead thunder of the sky-carrier's engines, the whole scene became loud with the sound of wailing sirens, and to complete the cacophony, another sector of his own alarms went off again, although Ancor was too far removed from the board to see from which quarter the new attack was being made.

Finally the cargo drop was completed, the cables were withdrawn, and the sky-carrier signalled away. Pausing only to close the deck of the reception pad, Ancor dashed below, to meet Sine Anura already coming up the stairs with a message. The officer directing the Zapoketa police operations wanted to see him immediately. Ancor gave Sine a set of crisp instructions, and then continued to the front of the building where he told the police quite pointedly that he was the victim of attack and sabotage. Seeing this was self-evident, the police immediately ran a strong cordon around the building, and began a search of Cherry's holo-theatre. Maq suspected that once a few intelligence operatives had been discovered, the effectiveness of the police would be quickly compromised, but for a while the scene grew relatively quiet and he was able to return to his own problems.

The new attempt at penetration, which had triggered the last set of alarms, had been made at the rear of the building. Here a minor window had been completely torn out, apparently by attachment to some vehicle in a delivery lane. Such was now the parlous state of his alarm system that it was impossible to tell if anyone had actually entered that way, nor was it important, because the window gave access only to the stores for Cherry's holo-theatre, and these all had locked steel doors which would prevent an intruder penetrating farther. The latest attack, however, had achieved its probable objective—the alarm system was now useless, and Ancor switched it off. He recognised that Varter was playing him at his own game of ultra security-consciousness, and that currently the fuzzy little man was winning hands down. Forced suddenly to consider the implications of the sequence of the night's events, Ancor's lionlike face became suddenly creased with comprehension. And the next instance he was running . . .

He was too late. Tez, discharged from his vigil in the corridor by a message delivered by Sine, had already released the bonded seals on the transit container, and he and Sine together were levering the great latch open. Ancor's imperative call to them to stop was entirely lost behind the loud slam of metal as the latch dropped free. The container's door immediately burst open and Imref Varter and a stranger Ancor supposed to be the one called Dil came out armed and dangerous.

"Don't anybody move, or we fire!"

Tez, taken completely by surprise, fell backwards off the low edge of the staging, and then rose awkwardly and frightened, with his hands above his head. Carli and Cherry, similarly scared, obeyed Imref's instruction to stand facing a wall with their hands well raised, whilst Dil covered Sine Anura with his weapon whilst they looked about for Ancor.

"Where's that damned assassin?"

"Here!" Ancor came in through the workshop door and he had weapons in both hands, one covering each of the intruders. "Have you any preference as to which of you I drop first?"

Imref Varter looked at the nervelessly steady weapon which pointed in his direction, and tightened his grip on his own, which was still pointing towards the quaking Cherry.

23

"You're bluffing, Ancor," he said, although he had private doubts about being able to re-target his own weapon within the response time available to a trained assassin.

Dil Carras was more positive. He stepped swiftly behind Sine Anura and jammed his weapon against her spine.

"Drop your weapons, Ancor, or she dies."

Ancor remained perfectly motionless, and there was no movement of his limbs or face which showed that he had even heard the demand. After a few moments of this impasse, Dil became insistent. He pushed Sine down the steps from the staging in order to position himself better for a shot at Ancor, and followed closely behind her, using her as a shield in case Ancor fired first. Having gained some valuable ground, Carras then took careful aim at Ancor's taut body, and said calmly: "The show is over, Ancor. Disarm or you're dead."

These were the last words Dil Carras ever spoke. Some slight movement by his unwilling hostage enabled her hands to barely brush his wrists. Instantly he fired, but was in the throes of such violent muscular contractions that his shot went up into the roof and the spasm of his own limbs threw him backwards like a broken doll on to the edge of the staging, where he lay and did not attempt to rise again.

Imref Varter regarded this incredible thing with a complete lack of comprehension for a second or two, then grinned wryly and threw his own weapon on the ground in front of Maq.

"I guess I made a mistake," he said ruefully. "Now tell me what you did to Dil."

Maq Ancor pouched his weapons and stepped down easily to pick up Varter's gun.

"Something you couldn't have known Imref. Sine Anura is an Engelian. She has an electromuscular system like an electric eel. Dil must have taken around six thousand volts through his arms and straight across his chest. Right across the heart."

"Is he dead?"

"Almost certainly, but you can check it out if you wish. Under such circumstances I think Sine would have given him everything she'd got,—it's not for nothing they call her Mistress Sin."

Imref Varter examined his comrade, and shook his head sadly, then looked up at Sine's green shining body. "A very deadly lady, in more senses than one. And I doubt if you're much less dangerous yourself, Maq Ancor. So what happens to me now?"

"Nothing," said Ancor. "You came in here to find out what was going on, and that's precisely what you're going to get—a conducted tour."

"And after?"

"You're free to go, of course. Had you but known, you need only have asked, and we'd have shown you anyway. We're attempting nothing illegal here according to your codes, and our reasons for shunning publicity are more in your interests than they are against them. Nor are we doing this for profit. In fact, the whole operation is costing us a tidy fortune."

"I already know that," said Varter. "But do you mean to tell me Dil and I went through all that exercise for nothing?"

"Worse than that, Imref. You already had the answers. It's just that you didn't believe them. Three times you've been to watch Cherry's holo-show *A Fantasy Journey Through the Universe of Solaria.*"

"I have, and I still can't figure out how you made those trick shots."

"That's because there were no trick shots. Every damn foot of that holo-tape was shot on location."

"You mean . . . ?"

"How much do you know about the Solarian universe, Imref?"

"I know that I live on the Saturn shell. Inside this I am told there are other gravitational shells, concentric ones inside the other, called Jupiter, Asteroid, Mars, and I forget the rest. Folklore has it that we in our turn are inside even greater shells called Uranus and Neptune, and so I suppose on outwards towards infinity."

"I wish I was sure of that infinity bit, but it's irrelevant for the moment. But can you tell me why all this is supposition, and none of it known for a fact?"

"Because we can't prove any of it. The only bridges between the shells are the shuttle spokes, and they only take emigrants outwards. Nobody ever comes back."

"The fact which we have been at some pains to conceal," said Ancor, "is that there is another route between the shells. When the shells are constructed by Zeus, the starting point is from a set of artificial worlds set in orbit around what will become the shell's equator. When the shell is finished, these worlds remain caged within the thickness of the shell, with a cavity called the interspace between them and the shell-mass itself. With a very special kind of exospheric ship it is possible to fly through this interspace around the cageworlds and visit other shells."

Imref's face registered doubt. "If that was so, why haven't we heard of it? Why have you kept it quiet?"

"Because some of the shells, like Jupiter, are vastly over-crowded. We daren't do anything which might trigger a massive unauthorised emigration. Unsatisfactory or not, only Zeus knows the population balance and the requirements on resources, and until we ourselves learn more about the dynamics and limitations of Solaria we daren't do anything which might tip the scales."

"And who is this altruistic 'we'?"

"We're from the Mars shell, where we've established a Centre for Solarian Studies. Those of us you see here are an exploratory team bound for an expedition out to the shell of Uranus and then to the Neptune shell and hopefully beyond into Hades-space. Because of the length of such a journey—over two thousand six hundred million miles each way, it was necessary to break the journey into two parts and build an interim camp here on the Saturn shell where we could re-stock our supplies."

"And that's what you're doing here?"

"Just that, and nothing more. We set it up to look like a reasonable commercial operation typical to the district, and we figured a bold front would attract less attention than one which attempted to conceal itself."

"You were right there," said Varter. "If you'd taken a backstreet warehouse, I'd have been in six months ago to see what it was you were doing. As it was, I'd already asked for this investigation to be called off as a waste of time."

"The point remains," said Ancor, "that when you walk out of here, precisely what are you going to do? Report us?"

Varter grinned ruefully. "You have me there! I'll have to make some sort of a report, but it'll be pretty negative. Do you think anyone would believe me if I gave it to them full strength? It would mean a quick trip before the medical board and a strong suggestion that I opt for premature retirement. I guess maybe I am past it, at that!"

"And what will happen about Dil?"

Varter looked at the fallen body on the floor and gave it an affectionate nudge with his twisted foot.

"What can I say about him? He had heart failure after a brief encounter with Mistress Sin. Knowing Dil and his habits, nobody in the department would regard that as being any more or any less than the truth. No, Maq Ancor, your secret's safe with me."

"Then I've a proposition," said Ancor. "We've an expensive installation here, but in a couple of days we must be on our way and leave it all behind. But it would be a pity just to let it go, especially as we shall be needing a halfway house on our return from Hades-space. Would you consider resigning from the service and taking over here as manager—Mistress Sin's, Cherry's holo-theatre, the lot? The installation is bought and paid for, so with reasonable diligence and acumen you could become a rich man in a very few years.''

"What me run a theatre and brothel?''

"Why not? For a man of your knowledge of the ways of life, it should be relatively easy.''

"My question was rhetorical. Of course I'll damn well do it. I'd be an idiot to refuse. But I'd like to keep in touch with the action itself, so my acceptance is conditional.''

"Upon what?''

"That you answer for me a question that's bugged me all my life—what the hell does happen to the emigrants who are taken off the Saturn shell?''

CHAPTER FIVE

Saturan

THEY DELAYED THE start of their journey for a few further days while details of the hand-over to Imref Varter were arranged. Originally they had intended merely to abandon the site and leave the authorities to ponder over the mystery, but the inclusion of Imref was a touch of genius, because it would relieve them of the necessity of having to repeat a similar exercise on their return. Finally, however, they were ready, the roof of the workshop was drawn back, and the little ship emerged from its lair in the centre of the city and shot without hesitation straight into the skies. Doubtless someone would complain about unauthorised low flying in the area below the wharf, but no explanation would ever be found, and the *Shellback*, heading directly into space, would soon be less than a chimera on the exospheric radar screens.

With the flight plan already set into the course computer, there was little that any of them had to do in the first few hours after take-off, and they gathered in the observation bay to watch the Saturn shell, which had been their home for many months, dropping slowly away beneath them. In all their journeyings, the leaving of a shell had become a ritual which none of them would miss. It was a lesson in relative size which no one who had experienced it could ever forget, and its great changes in perspective had a marvellous tonic effect which nonetheless coupled with a daunting realisation of the relative smallness of man.

They had started from a large workshop in a large street in a large city. Soon street and workshop had grown invisibly small, and the mighty sprawl of Zapoketa was itself contracting to become a minute point. At the same time, their area of view had opened up to include the surrounding land mass and the seas and the rivers of the region, and the great rib-like chains of bare-

28

backed mountains which stood out like a blue skeleton against the vast fawn and dun colours of a mighty agricultural belt. Slowly the blue skeleton shrank to become a miniature, a cameo, a spot, and fifty million square miles of growing wheat shrank to no more than a ragged handkerchief. So the never-ending contraction continued, with all the massive features becoming less and less distinct, and with only the forbidding brow of the horizon seemingly remaining as an unalterable constant.

Then they were into the luminary belt, carving a careful path between the bands of orbiting luminary proto-stars which lit and heated and gave life to the lands now so many, many miles below. Soon the brilliance of these artificial "suns" made it virtually impossible to see any further details on the surface of the shell, and all their eyes turned to the solitary feature which, like themselves, also rose from the Saturn shell—the great golden Exis spoke from Zapoketa, through which thundered a continuing sequence of freight and emigration shuttles *en route* to the shells of Uranus and Neptune, and hopefully beyond.

This spoke represented a feature which had fetched them so far and brought them the necessity to go so much farther. They had already travelled from the Mars shell inwards to the sun which sits at the centre of Solaria, and outwards finally to the shell of Saturn. Then Prince Land-a, who financed the expedition parties for the Centre for Solarian Studies, had come up with a curious question dredged out of the half-understood delirium of his shadowy liaison with the "mind" of Zeus itself. He had written much the same query as Imref had asked:

"Conjecture how we may, what do we really know of the fate of emigrants beyond the Saturn shell?"

Later, after another delirious empathic session with Zeus he had added a further enigmatic line:

"Who or what is the Tyrant of Hades?"

Nobody knew, and neither of these questions might ever have been answered, except that the *Shellback* was the one vessel in the known Solarian universe which had the capability to take the cageworld route right through to the surface of the Neptune shell and the space called Hades which lay beyond. This was the reason why Maq Ancor and his crew were now heading out beyond the Saturn shell, bound for a cageworld set in the shell of Uranus. They intended to find out what happened to the people who rode the shuttles in that great spoke.

Cherry was apprehensive. In order to span such extreme distances within a reasonable space of time, new motors had been fitted to the *Shellback*, aimed at considerably increasing its space-mode speed. Since the little ship was already the fastest

29

thing ever devised, there were no other vehicles available as a test-bed on which the engines could be tried, and thus he knew he was piloting a very powerful unit whose maximum capabilities had never been explored except in theory. Whilst they had already operated the motors up to over half their full potential, there was still no certainty as to what would happen when full power was applied, and the scrawny little man in sandals and white toga was genuinely shaking as he slowly built their space-mode velocity up towards the fabulous new target of half a million miles an hour. Even then, he knew it was going to be a long, long haul.

The spatial region between Saturn shell and the shell of Uranus had been designated Saturan-space by the Centre for Solarian Studies for the purposes of description. The calculations were that if Cherry could coax the *Shellback* up to its target velocity of five hundred thousand miles an hour, they could traverse the eight hundred and ninety-seven million mile separation between the two shells in a little over seventy-five days. One of the problems was that they had no means of knowing whether Zeus, as it had done before, had attempted any experiments in constructing useful habitats for man in this vast, empty region which it had at its disposal, and if something unexpected had been placed in their path, half a million miles an hour was a terrible speed at which to attempt to take avoidance action. Currently the radar warned them of a few large masses which were wandering in their sector of space, but none of these appeared likely to intercept their flight path, so they continued their watchfulness and maintained the slow wind-up of their speed.

Their communications with the Mars shell had been established through a careful chain of radio relays and repeaters, the last of which was built into the observation tower on the rooftop wharf of the building in the Liss-mal. Once they had penetrated really deeply into Saturan-space, this link would fail, and they would be without means of exchanging messages with the Centre for Solarian Studies until such time as they might again approach the Saturn shell. As the days passed and the signal strength began to fade, one of the last messages Ancor received read as follows:

SOO TO ANCOR: I HAVE HAD A PERSONAL INTER-VIEW WITH LAND-A ON THE SUBJECT OF THE TYRANT OF HADES. THE IMPRESSIONS HE RECEIVED FROM ZEUS WERE SO SUBJECTIVE THAT ANY ATTEMPT AT DE-SCRIPTION WOULD BE MISLEADING. HIS KEY WORDS ARE USURPATION, OPPRESSION AND CRUELTY, ALL OF WHICH ARE SEMANTICALLY EMOTIVE IN HUMAN

TERMS BUT UNLIKELY TO PROVOKE A REACTION FROM A MACHINE. YET LAND-A MAKES THE VERY TELLING POINT THAT HAD ZEUS' CEREBRAL CORE COMPLEX NOT BEEN GREATLY CONCERNED ABOUT SOME PHE-NOMENON IN THE NEPTUNE/HADES SECTOR, THESE IMAGES WOULD NOT HAVE BEEN AVAILABLE TO HIM IN THE FIRST PLACE. GUARD YOURSELVES WELL!

"What does all that mean?" asked Sine Anura. She had come into the computer bay a few moments earlier, and had been watching the slowly-filling screen over Maq's shoulder. Her heady scent made the air delicious.

"It means that Land-a still isn't sure what Zeus was worried about in Hades. But Soo is wrong about one thing. To a machine which has absolute control over human populations, usurpation, the illegal seizure of power, could be a very serious matter."

"But nobody could take population control away from Zeus."

"As far as we know, Neptune is one of the outer shells. That's frontier territory out there, without the benefit of all the centuries of establishment that the inner shells have had. I sup-pose that it is just possible that something or someone could have seized control of an entire shell."

"That still doesn't make it a problem. A lot of the Mars shell is controlled by the federation, but that doesn't bring it into conflict with Zeus."

"No. But then the federation, like the principalities, is firmly behind the principle of non-discriminative enforced emigration. But can you imagine, for instance, an entire shell where the Identifile was administered by a despotic government? What a marvellous way of ridding oneself of opponents and non-conformists if you selectively direct them to fill the emigration shuttles. There is no power that could not be yours."

"Do you think that is what might be happening?"

"There's too little evidence yet to take the speculation farther. But something appears to be wrong with Zeus' routines out there, and population balance has to be one of its prime objectives, because that's built into its first directive."

"But the second directive states that it should permit no actual or potential interference with the attainment of the first directive."

" 'Should' means that it must try, not necessarily that it will succeed."

"But it has such immense powers. For instance, it could withdraw all the luminaries, and simply let the whole place freeze over. No opposition could stand out against that."

"But such a move would affect the head-count, Sine, and that would run contrary to the first directive, so it couldn't do it. A dilemma like that could be calculated to run a mammoth cybernetic complex like Zeus right to the edge of its equivalent of a nervous breakdown—in which case there is less of a wonder that Land-a picked up some of the black-spots when he was having one of his sessions with Zeus."

She cradled his head in her hands, then stroked the folds of his complex face, marvelling at its animal ugliness. Knowing the deadly power she could deliver with her fingers by the merest trick of thought, Ancor knew that whilst she continued such caresses he was only a whim away from instant death, yet he leaned to her touch and welcomed it. Sine was an enigma, yet to him she was completely indispensable.

They might have progressed to a more passionate interlude, but a call from Cherry on the intercom interrupted them.

"Something I think you should look at, Maq. You know that large mass we were watching on the radar at the delta seven position?"

"I remember it."

"Well I turned an infra-red scanner on it, and it's hot."

"Hot?"

"Well, warm with hot spots. If I didn't know it to be impossible I'd swear it was a cageworld that's broken out of a shell."

"Complete with luminaries?"

"Too far to image yet, but the hot-spots could be luminaries, yes."

"Then break course, Cherry, and take us towards it. I want to have a look at it."

"It could add a further week to our journey, Maq, if we wind down again now. Is it that important?"

"I think so. It's always been postulated that a cageworld with satellite luminaries could exist as a free-space entity. It looks as though we might have the chance to examine one for ourselves. There is one thing we have to establish about it—does it or could it ever be made to sustain life."

"I think this is exciting, Maq," said Sine Anura. "There's something very appealing about the thought of a little lost world out there all on its own. I do hope there's life on it."

"So do I," said Ancor, stroking his chin thoughtfully. And there were visions in his eyes which went far beyond this little globe which sailed forlornly through the enclosed space of Saturan.

32

CHAPTER SIX

Corona

IN THE SUCCEEDING days, the image of the vagrant world grew slowly on the screens. By the use of image-intensifying techniques and computer manipulation of the received images, they slowly built up a picture of this strange wanderer in space. As Ancor had guessed, it was a typical cageworld, with a diameter of around eight thousand miles and a total surface area of about two hundred million square miles. Normally they would have expected to find it installed, complete with its orbiting luminaries, within the thickness of a major gravitational shell. How this one could have escaped from its "caged" position was very much of a mystery, and made the find all the more intriguing.

Finally they had it within range of the normal scanners, and the details were coming in beautifully. Seven ragged continents, giving a ratio of roughly half land and half water, had been set into a background of grey and impressive oceans, great chains of snow-capped mountains stood out like backbones across the major land masses, and where the heights slipped slowly into highlands they saw the unmistakable fringe of a tree-line and below that, belts of vegetation. This world, which they had dubbed "Saturan" after the space it occupied, was apparently very much alive.

But the presence of vegetable life—which was all that would be apparent from their still-extreme distance—did not necessarily mean that it would also have a human population. Ancor pored over his instruments trying to find some reading which might indicate that some form of population existed. There was a fair degree of radio transmission from the area, but all of it he judged to be random static from thunderstorms and the like, and he could find nothing which gave any positive evidence of the tenure of the world by man. It was completely possible, if this world had escaped from Zeus soon after terraforming and before a human component had been added, that the world would be fit for habitation and yet be uninhabited, and this was an interesting situation in a universe where living space was becoming such a crying need.

It was Sine Anura, watching the scanner screens with intense interest, who first pointed out the presence of the space machines. These were some of Zeus' own spacecraft, similar in form to the spacekeepers which fuelled and tended the luminaries, and were mainly in a very high orbit. The unusual factor was their number; no less than thirty of them apparently having been delegated to tend this one rogue world. The reasons for such concentrated attention were not obvious, for the same number of spacekeepers could easily have serviced a major shell. Ancor was caused to suspect that their presence had some extra purpose, but what that purpose was he could not even guess.

Slowly the instruments began to add to the visual detail. Gravitation, as deduced from the height and orbital periods of the luminaries, was substantially at the Solarian norm, surface temperatures were within the range of human tolerance, and there was an oxygen-nitrogen atmosphere of breathable composition. All the signs were that this world of Saturan had been engineered as a perfectly normal cageworld, and then unaccountably lost. But "lost" was not the right word. The presence of the space machines showed that Zeus was well aware of the location of the errant world, and it appeared content to give it a more than usual degree of attention. Was this some new living pattern being developed for Solaria—free worlds occupying the space between the shells? Ancor was intrigued, but the answers would have to wait until they made a close approach.

Slowly Cherry killed their space-mode speed, and finally they were in a situation from which they could consider making a landing. Everything the instruments had told them had been confirmed, and now the only things unusual about the world was the presence of the space machines and a high shiningness, a vague corona, which was present where the tenuous fringes of the upper atmosphere blended into the vacuum of space. Ancor pondered on the nature of this, but came to no firm conclusions, and, finding nothing which warned him to the contrary, he instructed Cherry to make a cautious touchdown.

It was as they approached the luminary belt that they first ran into trouble. The spacekeepers had obviously detected their coming, and moved with a swift unison to intercept their path. Such was

34

the size of these space vehicles and the accuracy of their placement, that Cherry had to abandon his first attempt and return again to their former position well out in space. Ancor went through his instrument readings once more, and finished up shaking his head.

"It would appear that there is something down there which Zeus doesn't want us to find, but I'm damned if I can see what it could be. Cherry, I want you to take us in again. Lay a straight descent course, then deviate on manual control at the last moment. The *Shellback* is a lot more manoeuvrable than a 'keeper, so it ought to be easy to dodge through."

Cherry summed the situation warily, then nodded his agreement and began to set a new heading into his controls.

"I don't like it, Maq. I don't doubt we can beat them, but it's a queer situation. They aren't attacking us, merely blocking. Could it be in our own interests that they won't let us go down?"

"The same thought had occurred to me. But there's only one way we'll ever be able to prove it, and that's to get through and find out. Just to be on the safe side, I suggest we use crash cocoons and safety harnesses while we go through, because there's obviously a factor here which we aren't seeing yet."

Ancor turned his couch in the computer bay so that he had a full view of the screens as Cherry began the new approach, and he watched the flowing figures intently, looking all the time for the first signs of the unexpected. Clenched in his fist was an emergency alarm trigger with which he could signal Cherry to abort the attempt if anything dangerous showed up. To his far right a scanner screen relayed Cherry's own view of the descent path, and on this it was already possible to see the spacekeepers positioning themselves for another attempt at blocking the *Shellback*'s way.

Cherry's manoeuvre was a masterpiece of deception. The descent path laid into the course computer was taking them on a broadly angular path, which necessitated the intercepting 'keepers having to match their velocity. Three spacekeepers were engaged in the interception, and having ensured that they were all moving fast and in the same direction, Cherry altered course right at the last moment to fall behind them. The 'keepers responded instantly, but such was their vast momentum that their powerful engines were unable to check their speed in time, and the *Shellback* was soon below them and itself checking velocity in order to avoid frictional heating when it hit the atmosphere.

Ancor, pinned to his couch by the inertial forces of the

sudden course change, watched the flowing figures on the screens, waiting for one of them to break away from the expected norm. Then, as they touched the tenuous edge of the world's atmosphere, the screen flared into a riot. Temperatures and pressures plunged upwards into the impossible, but more than that, a vast explosion literally took the little ship and hurled it back out into space again. Maq's decision to use the cocoons and harnesses was undoubtedly justified, because without this precaution they would none of them have survived, and they were a long way out in space again before Cherry recovered the ship from the automatic emergency-flight mode into which the mechanisms had thrown it.

"What the hell was that, Maq?" asked Cherry plaintively at last. "Did somebody swipe us with a missile, because I didn't see it coming?"

"Nothing came, else it would have registered on the instruments. No, it wasn't as simple as that. We got ourselves involved in some sort of reaction, and it took place at just about the level of that corona. Perhaps the corona is a reaction, a continuing one. But a reaction of what with what, I wonder. Tez, open up the weapons panel."

"Are we going to shoot at something?"

"No, but I want an unarmed missile case fired down towards that world there."

"But if it's unarmed, it won't explode. So where's the point?"

"But what if it does explode, Tez? What have we got then?"

Greatly mystified, Tez prepared a missile and saw it away, and then they all followed its progress on the scanning screens. One of the spacekeepers moved vaguely to intercept it, then apparently decided it was too small to bother with, and the device continued its downward descent towards the vague shining of the corona. Then there was the flare of an explosion so great that the scanner became overloaded and blacked out all the screens for a full half minute. When vision came back the corona had grown a giant sore "eye" where some heightened activity still continued, and the *Shellback*'s monitors had run almost to the critical range in recording the burst of heat and broad-spectrum radiations which the explosion had liberated.

"How does that work, Maq?" asked Tez at last.

"I can only theorize because I've no way I can test the assumption, but I think that entire world down there is composed of negative matter—that is matter composed of atoms in the normal way, but with the signs on the charges reversed. When

36

negative matter meets normal matter, the two annihilate each other, with the liberation of all the energy contained in both. We were very fortunate that we touched only the rarefied fringes of its atmosphere, because had we been able to penetrate deeper we'd have been destroyed completely. That corona is probably where the fringes of the negative-matter atmosphere is reacting with the occasional molecules from space."

Tez looked at the tranquil-seeming world depicted on the scanner, and shook his head in puzzlement.

"How would it get to be like that, Maq?"

"Again I can only theorize. We believe that the mass of material Zeus uses to build the shells and cageworlds is collected from some greater space outside Solaria, where it exists as immense clouds of dust and gas. By seeding parts of these clouds with gravitational centres, the seeds grow to become greater aggregates of matter, which finally compact themselves under the force of their own gravitational attraction. I think it possible that one of these clouds was a cloud of negative matter, and Zeus actually formed a cageworld out of it before discovering it was too dangerous to be situated in a normal-matter shell. So it pushed it out here where it couldn't do any damage, and left a few machines to guard it."

"I think that's rather sad," said Sine Anura. "A little lost world out here all on its own, which nobody wants and nobody can use."

"We aren't certain that nobody is using it," said Ancor. "Life-forms composed of negative matter are just as possible as life-forms composed of the more usual sort. Evolution could take place here just as it did on the one world which spawned the human race. Admittedly this world is a lot younger than the original, but Zeus must think it has potential, else it wouldn't bother to keep the luminaries in action. But there's one thing we can say for certain about any population which does arise there—no matter how hard they try, they're never going to make it into space!"

It was with a certain feeling of reluctance that they finally turned away from this sad and lonely little world. The space machines which guarded it paid them no further attention, and merely re-spaced themselves in their own high orbit as if waiting to warn the next attempting intruder. Ancor wondered just how long they would have to wait. As far as they knew, the *Shellback* was the only passenger-carrying spacecraft in existence, and probably the only vessel which had ever attempted to cross Saturan-space. Perhaps some day somebody in a craft which would need to be equally remarkable, would make the same crossing, and should its heading be comparable, it too might find the lost world of Saturan. Statistically, however, the odds were very much against it, and they had the feeling that theirs were probably the first eyes and the last to have seen it.

CHAPTER SEVEN

Inner Space

IT TOOK THEM a hundred days to reach the vicinity of the inner face of the Uranus shell, and they were all heartily tired of their confinement in the close quarters of the *Shellback* when Cherry began to reduce their space-mode speed. The Uranus shell was by far the largest they had ever visited, having an equatorial circumference of eleven thousand million miles—so large in fact that had they decided to fly right round it at the *Shellback*'s fastest ever speed, the journey would have taken two and a half years non-stop flight, and to do the trip by atmospheric aircraft would have occupied ten centuries. Even radio signals, travelling at the speed of light, would have taken around sixteen hours to circle the shell and return to their point of origin.

Ancor had to devise mental illustrations such as this to give himself a sense of scale, because the bare figure of one point one times ten to the power of ten miles, so suitable for the computer, psychologically conveyed almost nothing of the shattering enormity of the shell itself. Despite their speed and cleverness, the machines had never acquired a sense of wonder, and it took a human brain to read the marvellous into the mathematical exponent. Thus the figure for the total surface area of the Uranus shell was nearly four times ten to the nineteenth power square miles, but to Ancor, forty times a million million million was a figure which smote him with its unimaginable magnitude. Almost as difficult to imagine was the work of the tireless machines which had gathered from the clouds of some outer space sufficient material to construct a shell three thousand five hundred and sixty-six million miles in diameter and around six thousand miles thick.

Soon the scanners were clearly imaging the gaunt and sterile inner face of the shell. Without light, gravity, or atmosphere, this was a truly immense wasteland, having virtually the same area as the populated outer surface, but being completely uninhabited. The surface was of solid rock, which appeared to have been applied in a plastic, molten state from which it had contracted unevenly, leaving great whorls and depressions sometimes a million miles across, and the only relief to this awe-inspiring but depressing scene was the occasional pi-inversion generator terminal which maintained the impenetrable Exis planes which braced and divided the shell mass to prevent gravitational collapse.

According to calculation, the Uranus shell should have three hundred and seven cageworlds set around its equator, and it was to locate the nearest of these that Ancor was now scanning the surface. The volcano-like protrusion which led to the cavity containing a cageworld was around a thousand miles high and ten thousand miles across, but such were the massive natural features of the shrunken rock-face and the almost total lack of contrast that even a structure of this immense size was difficult to spot against such a terrifyingly large background. Scowling, Ancor re-started the scan in infra-red because the heat escaping from the surface of a cageworld through the aperture in the shell frequently betrayed its position. He found one ring-feature which superficially looked exactly like a cageworld aperture, but his scan told him it was completely cold, and he therefore disregarded it and went on with his search.

It was only after the ring-feature had been passed that the sudden arrival of a bright spot on his screen told him of the presence of something of higher temperature than the bleak rock of the shell. By comparison the hot-spot was very small indeed, and it was so unusual that he called Cherry's attention to it, and they brought the *Shellback* round for a closer look. From near-to, the ring-feature did have all the features of a typical cageworld aperture, but it was on the great slopes of this that whatever was warm was located. It was about the size of a medium town, but, being dwarfed so completely by the sheer mass of the "volcano," it was easy to understand how they had missed it on the first scan.

As they approached, the details became more apparent. Clinging to the almost vertical walls of the great mountainous protrusion was a whole series of rounded metal domes, interconnected by a regular grid of large "pipes" which were undoubtedly designed to form passageways between the various domes.

"It's a space-city!" said Sine Anura, as the image grew clear on the screens.

"It is, indeed, Sine. Which immediately raises the question of how did it get there? That stuff was made by humans, not by

Zeus, and they must have had to haul the whole lot from the shell's outer surface, which is the only place where it could have been manufactured. Just as interesting, why was it done?''

"And why build it down the almost vertical side of the mountain, Maq, when they could just as easily have built it on the horizontal?''

"I think the answer to that is that to them there's no difference. We're interpreting the scene with the *Shellback*'s artificial gravity to give us a reference as to what we consider horizontal and vertical. But there's effectively no gravity whatever on the inner surface of the shell, so anyone who lives in that city lives permanently in free-fall conditions.''

"Is it possible for people to live like that?''

"I've faith in the human body to adapt to almost anything. Yes, I think it would be possible. But the physiological changes which would take place would render it most unlikely that these people could ever again return to living under gravitational conditions.''

"Can we visit them?''

"We can ask if they'll permit it. But there may be practical problems of securing a vacuum-tight connection between them and the *Shellback* so that we can make the transfer. There's what I take to be a ship-grid and a space-lock up near the rim there, but at a guess their visiting ships are nearly the size of exospheric liners, and we can't match anything as big as that. The first thing we'd better do is try and make radio contact.''

Ancor turned his attention to sweeping the radio bands, trying to identify and frequency which was being used locally. There were several, but they were all carrying automatic telemetry signals, and did not respond to a voice call from the *Shellback*. Then he switched on the ship's own repeating call-signature, and very soon he got an answer.

"Hullo callsign *Shellback*! Identify yourselves, please.''

"We are a space-expeditionary party originating from the Centre for Solarian Studies on Mars shell. We are requesting permission to visit you.''

The conversation was halted by a string of oaths from the far end, and finally: "This is either a very expensive joke or the find of the century. Which are you, Captain?''

"We are no joke, believe me. We're just completing an eight hundred and ninety-seven million mile trip from the Saturn shell, and we were intrigued to find your installation here on the inner surface of Uranus. May we land?''

"Permission is being sought, Captain, but it may take a little time. Meanwhile you may approach our landing-grid and make fast. We will be in contact shortly."

"Why are you telling them all this?" asked Sine Anura, as Cherry brought the *Shellback* round. "Since they have exospheric ships they also have space-going potential. Isn't there a danger we'll trigger the type of population drift we sought to avoid on Saturn Shell?"

"There's always that possibility. But on Saturn shell we were attempting to conceal the fact that there was a route via the cageworld interspaces. These people obviously know the fact, else they couldn't have reached the inner face in the first place."

Cautiously they approached the metal landing-grid, which was obviously intended for the acceptance of exospheric craft many times the size of the diminutive *Shellback*. By means of gravlocks Cherry was able to secure their position near one of the great docking hatches, and then they settled down to wait. Shortly the message came.

"Hullo, *Shellback*! Permission for you to visit has been received . . . and welcome! To avoid the chore of matching transfer hatches, our engineers propose to draw your entire ship into a cargo-lock we can pressurize. Unfortunately we're on recycled air here, and should you be bearing any transmissible diseases we'd be highly vulnerable. So if you want to enter, it is on the condition that you remain suited and go through decontamination procedures. Is that acceptable?"

"Certainly!" said Ancor. "We ourselves have broadspectrum protective immunity, so you are not likely to affect us, but we respect your caution. Please go ahead with your arrangements."

Fifteen minutes later they had been drawn into the cavernous vastness of a cargo-lock, and the great seals had closed behind them. They had donned protective work-suits, normally intended for use in vacuum, and these felt tight and uncomfortable when they stepped out into the pressurized cargo-lock. Awaiting them was a crew with ultra-violet decontamination apparatus, with which the exterior of their work-suits was sterilised, and then they were permitted to proceed through a further lock and into the main installation itself. This was by no means the simple operation it appeared, because it was their first prolonged experience of free-fall conditions, which they normally only encountered on the *Shellback* when Cherry had to make some specific manoeuvre. Fortunately their hosts had had the forethought to provide them with a rope guide along which they could haul themselves, albeit untidily, to their destination.

Beyond the second lock were two men, who greeted them cordially.

"I am Buren Blumen, Chief Executive of our community here, and this is Makroom Dilpath, my assistant. Welcome to the space-community of Gaveen-Lyril! You must tell us about the Centre for Solarian Studies."

"Have you access to holo-projection equipment?"

"We can acquire some."

"Then better than talk about it, I'll make you a present of some holo-tapes, which will tell you both about the Centre and about ourselves and our wanderings through Solaria. The time we can remain in these suits is limited, and there is a lot we would like to know about yourselves before we have to return to our ship."

"I appreciate your urgency," said Blumen. "Come, let us travel while we talk. Gaveen-Lyril is very much of an experimental station as yet. We've no more than a thousand people here at the moment, but we plan this first city to hold a million. Then later we shall build a million cities, and so on until we populate the entire inside of the shell. Unfortunately it is not easy to adapt to living permanently in weightless conditions, and many who come here are forced to return. However, we are now seeing the second generation of those who have known nothing but free-fall all their days, and they would regard life with gravity with abhorrence."

The cargo-lock had been built into one of the great metal domes, and they had emerged from this into one of the interconnecting tubes. This was internally about fifty feet in diameter, and such were the conditions of weightlessness that the travellers had no means of knowing whether the shaft ran upwards, downwards, or horizontally. It was possible to imagine it as any of these, and if one thought of it as descending downwards, the effect was an instant dizzying sense of vertigo. Progress, however, was easy, because the walls of the tube were set with rings, which, providing it was remembered that lack of gravity did not cancel out momentum, enabled one to drift oneself from one ring to the next and thus proceed in any direction.

Whilst Ancor and his crew were cautiously finding their "space feet" under the amused eyes of Blumen and his assistant, there hurtled down the tube at breakneck speed three thin and light beings whose proficiency with traversing the rings was such that they need only touch one in a hundred, and thus appeared to be truly flying.

"These are the children of whom I spoke," said Blumen. "Our shell surface-gravity would crush them, because their bodies have never been adapted for it. But here they are completely in their own element—like fish in sea."

43

"Why was it considered necessary to populate the inner surface of the shell?" asked Ancor.

"Because something is wrong with the emigration program. It has not been increasing in proportion to the rate of growth of the population, and much of the shell's surface is grossly overcrowded. But here we have all the space we shall need for centuries. We have nuclear power for heat and light, our gardens make us self-sufficient for food, and our water, atmosphere and everything else is recycled. Our supply ships come daily from the outer surface at the moment, but one day we shall reach the position where we shall need nothing except the materials for further development."

The housing units were an unexpected dream, because they could be built right round a major tube, but it was a very curious sensation to see doors and windows up, down, to left and right, with the "street" an empty hollow running through the centre. Similarly with parks and gardens, the plants grew from a soft, foamed plastic matrix affixed all round the tube walls, with bright sunlamps set amongst them to illuminate those on the opposite wall. The central space was empty, and in it "swam" the lithe, graceful citizens of this surprising city on the inside face of the great shell of Uranus.

CHAPTER EIGHT

The Uranus Approach

ALL TOO SOON their suit monitors indicated that it was necessary for them to return to the *Shellback*. They had seen as much as they could of the installation in the time, and had found it very impressive. Already the embryo colony had become remarkably self-sufficient, and there was no reason they could see as to why the experiment should not grow and continue towards its promised aim of spreading over the entire inner surface of the shell. On their departure they gave Buren Blumen a set of holo-tapes which included Cherry's JOURNEY THROUGH THE UNIVERSE OF SOLARIA (with "fantasy" deleted from the title) and much factual information culled from the archives of the Centre for Solarian Studies.

Buren Blumen suited-up and came himself to look wistfully at the incredible *Shellback*, but it was plain that a journey of eight hundred and ninety-seven million miles through space was so far beyond the capabilities of Uranus shell technology that the prospect was merely a dream. Ancor was certain that after the Uranus shell authorities had absorbed the messages on the holo-tapes, although they might attempt a little exploration, a mass exodus was unlikely. Man was running into trouble right throughout Solaria, and a brief redistribution of populations would be of little gain to anyone in the long run. The overwhelming problem of where to find the fantastic volumes of new living space would still remain.

Then they took their leave. Soon the great cargo-lock had been evacuated of air, and the space-seals opened. They paused only while the moving ramps pushed them out on to the landing grid, then Cherry gently took control and thrust the *Shellback* back into Saturan-space for the next part of their journey. Their route was obvious: although there was something untypical about the cageworld aperture on which the city of Gaveen-Lyril was built, this was the way used by the exospheric ships which came from the outer surface of the Uranus shell, and where an exospheric ship could travel, the *Shellback* should have very little problem.

As they climbed towards the great rim, Sine Anura was thoughtful.

"Of all the people in Solaria, they're the first I've ever seen who have tackled the population problem for themselves. And what's more, they've solved it."

Ancor shook his head sadly. "I agree they've made a marvelous effort, and it should stand a few generations in good stead. Unfortunately it's only a palliative, not a solution."

"What do you mean, Maq?"

"Assuming they build a city to house a million, and for the sake of argument we then suppose they then bring in no more people from the outer shell. The population they've already established will double in thirty years, so in that time they'll need another city of the same size to house them all. Thirty years later they'll need four cities, then eight, and so on perpetually doubling up an exponential scale. In less than sixty generations that original million will have filled the entire inner surface of the shell to capacity, and the problem then is what the hell shall they do next? And all this mammoth effort has taken care of the descendents of no more than a paltry million of the billions upon billions who already occupy the outer surface of the shell."

"You're being very depressing, Maq."

"Sorry! But we have to be realistic. Human populations are currently doubling around every thirty years. It's probably taken man around one and a quarter million years to fill the universe of Solaria, but it will only take thirty years to fill a second one. The trouble is—there doesn't appear to be a second one available."

"But Zeus can always build more shells, and each is bigger than the last."

"I wish I shared your optimism. But all the evidence suggests that Zeus has reached some physical limitations out there somewhere, and can't go on producing new shells out to infinity. So the crisis which hit the one world where it all began is looming again, this time for all Solaria. We can buy a few centuries by filling in the gaps, but the basic problem is unresolved."

The annular rim of the great aperture leading to the cageworld cavity was two thousand miles wide, and its surface had been honed to flawless perfection by some unimaginable machines. The aperture itself was over five thousand miles across, and it was this they approached with great caution. The cavity within the thickness of the shell was maintained against the crushing pressures of the shell's mass by a spherical Exis field, open at each end. The cageworld, spinning around within a thousand miles of interspace inside the spherical field, was effectively insulated from the influence of the rest of the universe, and for practical and mathematical purposes the cageworld and its immediate environment were considered as a separate micro-universe on its own.

This was where the problems began. At the open ends of the Exis sphere, where were located the apertures which connected with the respective inner and outer faces of the shell, certain physical parameters of the micro-universe reacted with the universe outside. This gave rise to vast turbulences, manifest as temperature and pressure distortions, invariably located in the aperture just below the rim. These great physical storms were normally sufficiently violent to destroy any ordinary craft attempting to penetrate through to the cavity beyond, and it was to forge a passage through such regions that a craft like the *Shellback* had been specially developed.

As they swept over the edge of the amazing rim, Ancor began scanning the aperture, trying to determine the size and intensity of the turbulence in order to guide Cherry towards a safe passage. Then suddenly he began to understand how the people from the outer face of the Uranus shell came to be able to make the penetration to their inner-face colony of Gaveen-Lyril using ordinary exospheric ships—this aperture was different. No matter how much he searched, there was no turbulence to be found.

A second peculiarity became apparent almost immediately after. Where the cageworld itself should have been in sight, nothing was visible, nor did any mass register on the instruments. Advising Cherry to make the approach with caution, Ancor continued his scan, and finally he was satisfied with his conclusions. In this cavity there was no cageworld. Was this the "hole" from which the wandering world of Saturan had come? There was no way to prove it, but the probabilities were high.

No cageworld, no turbulence, therefore access from the outer shell-face to the inner could be gained using ordinary exospheric ships. The idea was feasible, but it also suggested a measure of the desperation of those who had conceived the necessity to populate the inner surface of the shell. A shell the size of Uranus should have had three hundred and seven cageworlds, and had many of these also become displaced into Saturan-space, the *Shellback* should have seen some of them on its long range scanners. In point of fact they had seen only one, and it was

47

probable that only one had been ejected into space. That meant that the inner shell had to be housed and populated through one hole only, and the logistics of this became appalling.

Ancor considered the proposition dubiously. It would take an exospheric ship forty-two years of non-stop flight to circumnavigate the inside face of the shell, and any lesser mode of transport could well take centuries. Unless whole existing populations moved continuously outwards, a new "settler" might grow old on the journey to the place where he was appointed to live, and supplies that could not be produced within the colony and had to be brought in from the outer face could easily arrive at some point in time to succour the grandchildren of the man who first requested them. Buren Blumen had mentioned that something was wrong with the emigration program for the Uranus shell. If Gaveen-Lyril was considered a solution, then the problem itself must be extremely bad.

They penetrated into the empty cageworld cavity without difficulty. Here was an immense spherical hole through the thickness of the shell, nearly ten thousand miles in diameter, and containing nothing but a vacuum slightly contaminated with molecules drawn from the atmosphere of the outer face of the shell. For the first time ever, Cherry was able to set a course which took them straight from one aperture towards the other without having to travel around an intervening cageworld, and they found the experience very peculiar indeed.

Within hours they had reached the great rim which led to the shell's outer face, and knew that in reality they were about to emerge from the giant volcano-like protrusion a thousand miles above the surface. Again they encountered no turbulence, and the sheer calm of their passage lent it an air of complete unreality. For the first time in such an emergence Ancor was able to abandon his instruments, and he joined Tez, Carli and Sine Anura in the observation bay to savour the dizzying experience as they swept suddenly over the rim's incredible edge, where a honed flatness of opalescent silica two thousand miles across, gave way reluctantly to the dun vagueness of the massive shell seen from a great height.

It was, indeed, the very tranquillity of the flight which caused Ancor to lower his guard, and within minutes he realised his mistake. Their leisurely traverse across the face of the great white rim, amazed by the perfection of its finish, was thrown into sudden confusion by the arrival of a dozen armed and wicked-looking exospheric craft which swooped from some even greater height to box the little ship against the glassy face. Ancor flew to the radio and tuned to the same frequency as he had used

48

when communicating with the space installation of Gaveen-Lyril. Shortly he had established contact.

"Space-vehicle *Shellback*, you are under constraint. We will send a ship ahead of you which you will follow down to landing point. Do not attempt to resist, or we shall be forced to open fire."

"This is piracy!" said Ancor. "We are merely passing through on a journey, and I have no intention of complying with your instruction. We are armed and prepared to resist. If you want to know more about us, contact your base at Gaveen-Lyril which we recently visited."

"It was what Gaveen-Lyril told us that forced us to the decision to intercept you. You have true space engines and must have a powerplant to suit. Our need to develop both of these things is so urgent that we daren't let ethics or diplomacy stand in our way. We intend to have your ship, Captain, to take it apart and see how it works. Co-operate, and you will be well looked after."

"There are many reasons why I can't accommodate you," said Ancor. "But firstly, this ship is engaged on a mission which I intend to complete. Secondly, the possession of such space-going capability by an overcrowded major shell could lead to a serious disruption of the population balance throughout all Solaria. Irrespective of your overpopulation problems, I cannot be responsible for handing you the key to mass migration across inter-shell space. Call off your ships, and leave us in peace."

"I'm warning you, Captain!"

"Don't be stupid," said Ancor. "You could only lose."

During the conversation, Tez had opened up the automatic weapons control panel, and the multiple screens now showed each of the intercepting craft locked under the crossed hairs of the sighting graticules. Then one of the attackers launched a missile. This was not targeted on the *Shellback*, but aimed at a point ahead of the little ship, and obviously intended as a frightener. The device never reached its destination. The *Shellback*'s own anti-missile defences destroyed the missile before it had completed half its journey. The second missile, this time aimed directly at the little ship's hull, came uncomfortably close, but was destroyed just in time, and it was the ship which had fired the weapon which became the centre of a frightful flare as Tez's response salvo found its inevitable target.

They had by now reached the edge of the great rim, and Cherry suddenly had an open thousand miles below in which to attempt to break out of the box. As they cleared the mountain he both dipped and accelerated the *Shellback*, forcing a power dive which was clearly beyond the capabilities of their attackers. Seeing the break-away manoeuvre, the other ships in the exospheric fleet also responded to the order to open fire, and for several hair-raising minutes the whole sky was ablaze with the flare of missiles and counter-missiles, and the vast light of several exploding powerplants.

Finally Cherry pulled out of his dive and took the *Shellback* up almost vertically into space. The radar showed the attackers now fallen far behind, and only six blips marked the positions, where there had formerly been twelve. The battle had been won not so much by Tez as by the automatic weaponry with which the little ship had been so fortunately provided. Ancor looked back gravely at the damage they had wrought, and regretted it had cost the lives of men, but the skirmish had not been of his choosing, and somewhere ahead, still over a thousand million miles away on the Neptune shell, the tyrant of Hades was waiting.

CHAPTER NINE

The Choice

"LEVEL HER OFF, Cherry."

"What?"

"I still want to see what the surface of the Uranus shell looks like. These people have been driven to two extremes—building Gaveen-Lyril, and attempting to capture the *Shellback*. Obviously they're facing population pressures of the most shattering kind. I want to go down there and see for myself."

"After what we've just done to them? We shot down six of their ships, remember?"

"That was their choice, not ours." Ancor returned moodily to the radio and began calling. "This is Mars shell vessel *Shellback*, representing the Centre for Solarian Studies. Will somebody patch me through to Buren Blumen, commanding Gaveen-Lyril."

He put the call on tape and let it repeat endlessly, whilst he searched the wavebands for an answer. Then he received an acknowledgement from a relay station, and half an hour later Blumen's own voice came over the link.

"Captain Ancor, a million apologies! We had to report your coming, but we never dreamed they'd attempt an armed interception. Some local commander took a snap decision which was most unwise."

"So unwise that it cost them six ships."

"I'm surprised they got away so lightly. Any vessel which can do what yours has done is hardly likely to fall to the attack of ordinary exospheric craft. We've been running some of your holo-tapes, and I think now that I can see what you were trying to say. It isn't just Uranus shell which has a population problem, it's a problem becoming shared by all Solaria. All we can sensibly do by building Gaveen-Lyril is to buy ourselves a little extra time. The ultimate problem still remains."

"And it was to attempt to comprehend and resolve such problems that the Centre for Solarian Studies was established. It's to understand our universe and what is happening to it that we on the *Shellback* make these explorations. But because of our skirmish, we're lacking critical data on the whole of the outer face of the Uranus shell. We want to land to add to our records, and we want guaranteed immunity from attack whilst we do so."

"I think I can promise you better than that, Captain Ancor. Such are the distances on the shell that our higher authorities have only just learnt of your arrival and the scandalous way you were treated. It's not every day we receive visitors from another shell. I think for you they will kill the fatted calf and arrange a reception fit for heroes."

"The ceremony we could do without," said Ancor. "But access to a few computer data banks relating to social structures would be useful."

"I would think that would be the least of what they will give you. Your arrival must be one of the most momentous events in the history of the shell. Please maintain your position and keep this channel open. We shall speak again."

This time with a milder escort of commercial exo-craft which kept a discreet distance, the *Shellback* levelled at last over the incredible cities of the Uranus shell. Used as they were to the sight of hyper-conurbations, this one left them gasping. They were over a skyscraper city, but few, if any, of the gigantic needles of steel and glass which reached towards the sky could have been less than a mile in height, and strange and dizzying was the maze of intermediate walkways and traffic tubes which spiralled and leaped between the staggering towers.

"A mega-megalopolis!" said Sine Anura in wonder.

"And so densely populated that they haven't been able to build it beneath the fields, as they do on some of the other shells. Which is a grave limitation. It isn't space which ultimately limits a population's growth, because you can always stack people vertically. Your final limit is your ability to capture the radiant power from the luminaries to fuel the ecological system. Like it or not, ultimately we are all radiation eaters."

"There were no luminaries on the inner face of the shell, Maq," objected Sine. "Yet they plan to expand Gaveen-Lyril and have people living there."

"True, but they're using the only other source of power there is—nuclear. But it's a limited option. Once all the available nuclear fuel is spent, there is no way of replacing it. Certainly it

52

may last them for quite a few centuries, but at the rate they're planning to use it, I doubt if they'll get the inner-shell installation finished before they run short of the fuel to power it.''

"Do you think they don't know of this?"

"Of course they do. Any of their engineers could calculate it. But I'd say it was politically expedient not to let the facts be known. To the lay public, the promise of forty million million million square miles of habitable territory must seem like the answer to any overpopulation problem. And there's the illusion.''

The folds of Ancor's lionlike face were moving, each seeming to be motivated by a separate pattern of thought, and his eyes were looking at visions which lay far beyond the marvellous city and its mile-high towers.

"Where's the illusion?" asked Sine. "You're talking about one hell of a lot of space there.''

Ancor turned his attention back to her, and his eyes were grave.

"Look at it this way, Sine. Assume they're already occupying a similar amount of territory on the outer face of the shell, and the population doubles every thirty years. Then in thirty years they'll need the whole of the inner face of the shell. And what the hell will they need in sixty years? For all its brave concept and technology, Gaveen-Lyril is mere political pap.''

They were invited to land on an exospheric pad in the centre of one of the largest landing fields they had ever seen. Alerted by local newscasts, the population had turned out in massive numbers, the observation terraces were packed to suffocation, and it was difficult to imagine that the major highways could have accommodated even one extra person. They were met by a small, wheeled vehicle, driven by a uniformed officer, who saluted smartly and explained that they were to be taken to a special reception. The regional president, it seemed, was also already on his way.

Seeing the throng on the roads, Ancor wondered by what form of magic they were to be conveyed anywhere, because in no way could a vehicle have been forced through the crowds. At the edge of the field, however, it became apparent that there was a special system of roads and bridges reserved for police, military and administration purposes, and the public had no access to these at all. Whole levels of the buildings through which the high roads passed were similarly reserved for those concerned with population control, and they gained the uncomfortable feeling that the "establishment" had gone to great lengths to separate itself physically from the community it was in theory meant to serve. The incidence of armed police and guards was a potent pointer to the fact that not all the population regarded this situation as acceptable, and they could only guess at the horrific power struggles which must take place for the control of the administration.

They arrived finally at a large hall, where they were introduced to a great number of "chairmen" and dignitaries, all, it appeared, in government employ, and with whom they finally sat to partake of a splendid meal. Shortly after the meal ended, however, there was an interruption. The regional president himself had finally arrived, and he strode into the hall without any pretence of ceremony or protocol.

Ancor summed him interestedly. The man was not at all what he had expected. Tall and dark, dressed exclusively in black and with a cloak that flared like flying wings, the man's face was shrewd, intellectual, and completely ruthless. He was a Machiavellian prince, a natural ruler, and his ways had nothing to do with those of the sycophants and power-seekers around him. He strode up to Ancor, and having ascertained that the latter had finished his meal he merely beckoned and said: "Come!"

Ancor followed him to a private room, and the dark man turned abruptly.

"During the flight, I've been in touch with the Executive of Gaveen-Lyril. From what he has gleaned about you from your meeting and your holo-tapes, I think I can judge the type of man you are. So I'll dispense with the formalities and come straight to the point. I expect you to be as direct with me."

Ancor did not answer, but the question was sufficiently rhetorical that no reply was needed. Without delay the president continued.

"As a man of the universe, Ancor, what do you think of our Gaveen-Lyril experiment?"

"It's a toy, a political expedient."

"Should we continue with it?"

"Of course. It will buy a few extra generations for a few millions. But in the face of your coming crisis, that will be a mere drop in a very great ocean."

The president stiffened. "I said nothing about a crisis."

"You didn't need to. Physics decrees you have a crisis. With the level of incoming radiation, you can grow only just so much food, no matter how good your husbandry. When the demand for food exceeds that precarious supply, you have a crisis."

The president examined him narrowly for a moment, then said: "I was right about you, Ancor. You are a man of the universe. So what's the answer?"

"As yet there is no answer. We don't yet know what is going

54

wrong with the emigration program. We don't even know if the program can be continued in the face of suspected limitations to the growth of Solaria."

"I meant what is our answer, not the universal answer."

"You don't strike me as a man who suffers having his decisions taken for him," said Ancor. "There are two remedies for gross overpopulation, war and famine, both with long and discreditable histories. From what I've seen of the strength of your administration, I take it you have the choice between them."

"Aye! I have the choice. I rather sought for you to bring me something in the nature of hope."

"I wish to God I had it with me to bring. History records that once there was but one populated world in the universe, and that too became greatly overcrowded. Somehow they managed to make themselves a second world, then soon they needed four, then eight. Later, in partnership with Zeus, they started the construction of the shells. The staggering increase in living space which the shells gave them must have seemed like an end to the overpopulation problem for all time. But the vicious reality of exponential growth is that man now fills all the shells of Solaria, and the old crisis is back with us. Where can we find another universe? And how long would it last us if we did?"

"You comfort me, Ancor," said the president suddenly. "I thought I bore all the burdens in Creation. But I see now there are some with crosses even heavier than mine. I know now what I have to do."

"Don't torment yourself with decisions," said Ancor. "If you do nothing at all, the results will be similar. History will use you as its instrument, but it is history which is infamous, not the man."

Later, Ancor and his crew returned to the *Shellback*. In their absence a high-speed data link had been transferring statistical details about the Uranus shell's populations into the little ship's data banks. The stories these told were amazing. So seriously inadequate had the emigration program become that the average population density on the habitable land-mass was an astounding hundred thousand persons per square mile, ten times the Solarian norm. In order to leave land available for critical agriculture, most of these people were concentrated into the vast mega-megalopolises, where the living densities were such that had it not been for the vertical separation afforded by the mile-high towers, the entire area of the cities could have been filled solidly with bodies packed tightly together and seventy people deep.

Ancor wrote down the figure two and after it added twenty-four zeroes. It stretched right across the page. This was the approximate number of people alive on the Uranus shell, and every one of them was an individual, precious and unique. The president's problem was that only a finite amount of energy was available to power the ecology, and every second a thousand million million new mouths were being added to the burden. Whether he acted or not, the whole system was on the verge of mammoth breakdown, and literally billions would have to die in order that those who remained might live.

CHAPTER TEN

The Eye of Nepturan

THIS TIME ANCOR did not look back as the *Shellback* began to claw its way into space. In his mind's eye the Uranus shell's face was already bright with the flare of a thousand nuclear weapons, and this was a nightmare which pursued him even though he was awake. Probably it would not happen this way. Perhaps the population would become self-limiting by the slower process of starvation, but whatever form it took, massive death was to become an inevitable reality for the population of the Uranus shell, and Ancor was crying inside.

As usual it fell to Sine Anura to try to break him out of his mood, though it took all her skills in erotic artistry to do it. Later, when she had him calm and rested again, she said to him: "You can't do it, Maq. You can't take the cares of all Solaria on your own shoulders. That's why Zeus was invented—because the problem was too big for men to handle it."

He stroked the green shiningness of her naked flesh appreciatively, and gave a tired smile.

"I know it, Sine. But to Zeus we're just cyphers, digits to add up to justify the head count. It takes a human being to recognise that every human being is unique and marvellous. It takes a human being to recognise suffering, and to care about things like war and famine. Zeus is many millions of times cleverer than man, but it doesn't actually care."

"We don't know that for certain, Maq. Perhaps in its own way it does care. If not, why does it dream?"

"Dream?"

"The empathy it shares with Land-a. The tyrant of Hades— whatever that might prove to be—is some sort of nightmare or a dream. There's something out there even Zeus can't handle, and it's bugging it. I think that's because Zeus does care."

"Remind me one day to explain to you about artificial intelligence, and how little it has to do with the ordinary human kind of thought."

"I don't care what you say, Maq. When you consider the billions upon billions of human beings in the Solarian universe all being housed and fed on resources provided by Zeus, you know it has to have a feeling for its task."

"On the contrary, it's merely responding to its program."

"I think once it may have done, but now it's outgrown those crude and early inputs. I think now it responds to its own motivation, based on . . . how can I explain it?"

"Based on what, Sine?"

"Dare I say it . . . love!"

He laughed and kissed her, and finally fell asleep with the idea still in his mind. And when he awoke, the idea did not seem so ridiculous at all.

The region between the Uranus shell and the shell of Neptune had been designated Nepturan-space by the Centre for Solarian Studies. The journey between the two shells was a space voyage of one thousand and ten million miles, which was quite the longest single hop the *Shellback* had ever undertaken. Even at their enhanced space-mode speed, the journey would take them all of eighty-five days, and the prospect of spending three months in the crowded confines of the little ship was not at all appealing. However, they were on the last major step of their journey, and there was a growing feeling of tension, because somewhere ahead of them, probably on the face of the Neptune shell under the region of space called Hades, was something or somebody which appeared to worry even Zeus itself.

There had been virtually no information whatever established by the Centre for Solarian Studies about the Neptune shell or the Hades-space region, apart from a brief figure for the shell's presumed distance from the sun, and Ancor's request for information from the ship's computer was not very rewarding.

NEPTUNE SHELL: BELIEVED TO BE BASED VERY APPROXIMATELY AT THE MEAN ORBITAL DISTANCE OF A FORMER SOLAR SATELLITE CALLED NEPTUNE, WHICH WAS ITSELF PROBABLY DESTROYED DURING THE CONSTRUCTION OF THE SHELL. CALCULATED RADIAL DISTANCE FROM THE SUN 2793 MILLION MILES. SEE STANDARD TABLES FOR PROJECTIONS OF OTHER CRITICAL DATA. IN CLASSICAL MYTHOLOGY, NEPTUNE WAS KING OF THE SEA. HE MADE LOVE TO AMPHITRITE AS A DOLPHIN, AND ASSUMED OTHER SHAPES FOR SIMILAR DECEPTIONS.

"Sounds like a good match for Sine," said Ancor to himself.

HADES: TENTATIVE NAME GIVEN TO THE SPACE RE-GION ABOVE THE SURFACE OF THE NEPTUNE SHELL. THEORY PREDICTS ANOTHER SHELL ENCLOSING THIS SPACE, CALLED PLUTO SHELL, BUT THE EXISTENCE OF THIS IS UNCERTAIN. IN CLASSICAL MYTHOLOGY, HADES WAS THE GOD OF THE UNDERWORLD, AND THE NAME IS ALSO GIVEN TO THE INFERNAL REGIONS.

"None of this encourages me in the least," said Ancor, turning aside to follow more practical pursuits.

On previous expeditions they had frequently encountered ac-tive opposition from Zeus to their free movement through the regions of Solaria. The fact that they had not done so on this trip had the possible interpretation that Zeus itself welcomed human intervention from another shell into whatever problem sat below Hades. Such ideas were not to be taken as an assurance, however. Because of the distances involved between shells and around the girth of the shells, Zeus had established a number of semiautono-mous "executive" centres to regulate local affairs such as emigration, the control of the spokeways, and the tending of the orbiting luminaries. With Zeus, in its world-sized complex in the Venus shell, now more than two thousand million miles away, the shortest time in which a query from a local centre could possibly reach Zeus was three hours, and six hours would elapse before a decision could be received back.

With the tight control Zeus exercised over the movement of people throughout Solaria, it was entirely possible that some local executive centre would react against the freemoving *Shellback*, and even if Zeus chose to countermand the action, such an instruction would be six hours late. Ancor had no intention of allowing a false sense of security to make him relax his guard, and as the little ship bored its way through Nepturan-space, every available scanner and detector was being employed to its fullest extent to search the mighty wastes for any possible signs of trouble. As far as they could tell, the space region was empty, but periodically Ancor sent a torpedo directly ahead down their flight path and tracked it by radar to ensure that not even something unseen lay hidden in their way.

They had progressed thus for nearly half of the journey, and were better than forty days out from the Uranus shell, when something happened which was so utterly inexplicable that had they not seen it for themselves they would never have believed it. The radar and all the electronic surveillance gear remained silent, but those instruments sensitive to light warned suddenly of something strange in the region of perfect darkness into which they were heading. Ancor leaped to his scanners immediately, received no image at all over most of the radiation bands, and it was only when he re-scanned in the narrow bandwidth for the visual spectrum that a picture came. When he saw it, his astonishment was great.

For out in the midst of the great wastes of Nepturan-space there hung a huge and solitary eye.

His impression was confirmed by Sine Anura, who had been exercising in the observation bay. She gave a little shriek and fled to where Maq sat amazed before his instruments. Her brief glance at the screens showed her that he was already aware of the phenomenon.

"What the hell is it, Maq? How can you have an eye out there in space?"

"The answer is that you can't, Sine. That thing is larger than a cageworld, yet it looks like . . ."

". . . a living, human eye," she said.

"That's exactly what it looks like." He was already checking his other instruments rapidly. "But it's completely insubstantial. No mass, no matter, no nothing. Get Cherry up here. I want to know if that's some sort of holo-projection."

Roused from his sleep, Cherry's first reaction was one of complete incomprehension. He stared stupidly at the image on the screens for about a minute, then went down to the observation bay to see it with his own eyes. Suddenly fully awake, he called for Tez, who came with a battery of polarising filters and various meters and began to make some tests. Finally a perplexed Cherry came back to Ancor.

"No terrain hologram that, Maq. It's actually out there."

"But there isn't anything out there," said Ancor, beginning to be exasperated. "The rest of the electromagnetic spectrum is entirely clear. The image is all there is. And I'll tell you something else—it's aware of us."

"How do you figure that?" asked Sine.

"Our present velocity is around half a million miles an hour, yet that thing stays at the same apparent distance from us. In other words, it's being withdrawn at a pace which exactly matches our real speed. That's a nice piece of technology, and it isn't happening by accident."

"Does everything have to be done by technology? Couldn't whatever it is be supernatural?"

"I don't happen to believe there is any such thing as the supernatural, and even if there was it would be a pretty negligible force when compared with the powers of micro-electronics. Tez, can you get a weapons-range on that thing?

"I already have it, Maq."

"Then put a diffract-meson warhead on a space torpedo, and aim for the centre of that pupil. I want to see what it does."

"Arming torpedo now," said Tez.

"Fire at will."

Starting with the velocity at which it was being carried by the ship, and with its powerful propellant driving it smoothly to an even greater speed, the torpedo surged ahead of them, and they all watched breathlessly as it swooped towards the centre of the eye. Just before the missile reached its projected point of impact, the eye did an amazing thing. It blinked. Then the whole image was lost against the violently curling flare of a diffract-meson explosion at relatively close range. All the detection instruments on the *Shellback* screamed in unison as the little ship overtook the epicentre of the explosion and for a few moments was immersed in a cloud of ionised contaminants which filled the vacuum with bright and insubstantial fire.

When the screens cleared again, the eye was still there, but drastically altered. A great black crater had been formed in the former glassy surface of the pupil, and the vast white rim was suddenly shot with the red veins of acute pain. Then suddenly it was gone, as though an eye which had been applied to a spyhole had been hastily withdrawn.

"Well, I still can't figure what it was," said Ancor. "But obviously we hit it. Though how one can hit something which isn't even there, is something of a mystery."

"I remember once," said Sine, "you showed me one of those trick gadgets where you place something in a reflecting bowl, and an insubstantial image of the object forms above it. I think you called it a three-dimensional real image."

"Yes, and I think I see where you're leading. That could just have been a three-dimensional real image of an actual eye with some vast magnification thrown in. But that doesn't explain how we managed to hit it with a diffract-meson warhead."

"But we wouldn't need to hit it, Maq. We created a fireburst at the focal point of the optical system, and this was focused back by the optics to burn the actual eye itself. Just as if the real eye had been hit by a laser."

Ancor turned to her with genuine admiration.

"Do you know, I think you've hit it, Sine! That was some form of spyhole on space—a form of reflecting telescope through which somebody was watching our coming. We fired at the image but damaged the original, as a man can blind himself by focusing a telescope on a luminary. But do you realise what we're dealing with here? That technique was a full order of technology above anything we've encountered elsewhere in Solaria—and I don't think it was any coincidence that we met it on our run up to the territory of the tyrant of Hades.

CHAPTER ELEVEN

Fire-Pit

FOR THE REMAINING seven weeks of flight they saw no further signs of the eye, but occasional swirls of unexplained luminance in the ether suggested that perhaps the human organ had been replaced by optical instruments applied to the eyepiece of the system. When one of these vaguenesses persisted in view for a few hours, Ancor exploded another diffract-meson warhead against the insubstantial image, and was rewarded with the sight of a vast crack which spread across the sky. Thereafter they saw no further signs, but it was still possible that a means had been found for them to continue to be found but without the observing mechanism itself becoming visible. It was, however, a curious sensation to think that their progress might be being closely watched for every second. As Sine said: "It's rather like living under a microscope."

Ancor had been trying to guess what sort of optical instrument had been trained upon them. Which ever way he made the calculation, the formation of a real image in their vicinity required a reflector of truly amazing size, and he was hard-put to explain how a mirror of such incredible dimensions and perfection could possibly be made. His final conclusion was that it could only be achieved by the use of a hemispherical Exis field, somehow rendered highly reflective, and this notion raised its own problems. Only Zeus had access to equipment which could create an Exis field that big—and Zeus did not use human observers! Something incredibly strange was taking place on the Neptune shell.

Indistinct at first on the long-range scanners, the inner face of the Neptune shell had slowly come into view, and the detail increased as they approached. Its form was similar to that of the other shells, bare and sterile rock randomly shrunken into great

63

whorls and depressions, but this one contained an unusually high number of Exis-plane generators to support and separate the shell mass. This feature suggested that the shell had been created and was being maintained only with the greatest difficulty against physical forces which were threatening to drag it apart. They did not know if this was the outermost shell of Solaria or how many others might have been formed around it, but it was obvious that the engineering systems which had given such stability to the inner shells were proving less satisfactory near the outer limits of Solaria.

In vain Ancor hunted for trace of the reflecting telescope which had been used on them, but there was no sign of it, nor was it reasonable to expect it to be located at the point of the shell at which they had arrived. He turned his attention then to considering the details of the shell itself. Its proportions were massive. Its circumference he found to be over one point seven times ten to the power of ten miles, and had they chosen to fly right round it at their fastest speed, the journey would have taken four years. It was nearly impossible for a human mind to convince itself that such a staggering area could ever become fully populated, apparently having such limitless territories to offer. However, the relentless truth behind the growth of populations which doubled every thirty years was that Adam and Eve could have filled the habitable land-mass with ten thousand people to the square mile in only a little over two and a half thousand years.

Having established tentative figures for the shell's size by observing its radius of curvature, Ancor then started to scan for a cageworld aperture which could give them access to the outer face. His calculations told him that there ought to be four hundred and eighty cageworlds around the equator, but although the aperture protrusions were massive in any human terms, they were dwarfed into insignificance by the startling immensity of the shell itself and the massive random features of its rocky surface.

Also of interest were the Exis spokes which spanned the gulf between the shells, some of which were filled with a continuing sequence of high-speed shuttles carrying emigrants. Others, and there was no way to determine which, were carrying a very restricted flow of shuttles, and these were the ones which originated primarily at the surface of the overcrowded Uranus shell. All of them plunged into and through the shell of Neptune, some supposedly to terminate there and some to continue on out towards the outer reaches of Solaria. This was the system on which all the inner shells relied to prevent being choked to death by the pressures of their own increasing populations; and this was the system which, somewhere ahead of the *Shellback*'s path, had gone dramatically wrong.

As he scanned to try and determine an approach course for Cherry, Ancor also had all his other detectors in full operation. The message of the eye in space had not been lost on him. Somebody knew they were coming, and that somebody had access to some pretty rare technology. He could afford to overlook nothing. There were several radio transmissions fanning out on broad beams being directed to adjacent parts of the shell, but these appeared to be automatic monitoring signals of some sort, and were probably concerned with co-ordinating the Exis-plane generators which braced the shell. Activity in the rest of the electromagnetic spectrum was relatively low, nor could he find any indication of the presence of space machines or spatial objects which might be dangerous. Yet while his instruments told him nothing to cause him concern, he could feel a tension building in his own body. Instinctively he sensed the jaws of some dynamic trap, but search as he might he was unable to find it.

A scan in the infra-red band finally located the heat leakage from a cageworld set into the thickness of the shell. This was so far distant that it necessitated an additional three days' flight, and calculation suggested that there should have been one nearer. Ancor, however, opted to go towards an established feature rather than continue his tedious scanning of the millions upon millions of square miles of randomly-scarred rock in search of one which was proving remarkably difficult to locate.

In the hours of their approach Ancor carefully studied the aperture and its surroundings, looking for something which might confirm the uneasy feeling which had beset him. From the amount of radiant heat which escaped from the giant volcanic rim, he judged that the cageworld itself must be very hot, which was unusual because their temperatures were normally maintained well within the range of human tolerance. Not all cageworlds, however, were fit for human habitation, and Zeus had itself experimented with the breeding of mutated human strains for populating fringe conditions. It was possible that this was yet another cageworld which had failed to meet its specification, and there was nothing necessarily sinister about the "hot" world which apparently occupied the cavity.

Hovering over the rim, they carefully probed the aperture. Here they found a fine-grained turbulence, which was largely what they had anticipated. The pressure and temperature differences in the "granules" were extreme, but they had become used to shorter period and more-violent turbulences the farther outward they travelled through Solaria. The turbulent effects were such that they could gain no direct imagery of the cageworld itself, but their readings amply confirmed the very high temperatures of the cageworld and its attendant luminaries.

"Do we go for a penetration?" asked Cherry.

Ancor looked up from his instruments. "Something tells me that we shouldn't. But I can't actually find anything wrong. So I suppose we'd better go—but cautiously."

"We can't penetrate cautiously," objected Cherry. "There's an optimum speed for making a penetration, dependent on the granular size of the turbulence and the necessity to kill our velocity before we get too deeply into the atmosphere below. We either go, or we don't."

"All I'm saying, Cherry, is that if something goes wrong when we hit that mess down there, we have to be prepared to pull out again fast."

"And I'm saying that I'll probably kill us all if I attempt such a course change in mid-manoeuvre. Honestly, Maq, you know the kind of velocities we're playing with. A limited amount of artificial gravity we have, but artificial inertia has yet to be invented."

"Sorry, Cherry! I know you're right. But I've the oddest feeling about this exercise. Let's compromise. Lock-in an emergency-flight mode which will fetch us back out into Nepturan-space should you lose control for any reason."

"I've never mentioned it before, Maq, but I always go for a penetration with an emergency back-off mode preset."

"Then you're a jump ahead of me. I've only just realised what a wise precaution it could be."

At the minimum speed calculated to ensure safe passage through the turbulence, Cherry set the little ship to its task. Carli, Tez and Sine were relatively safe inside their crash cocoons, Cherry was strapped in his control cockpit, and Ancor had affixed himself to the safety couch in the computer bay. Then, with the course entirely under the control of the ship's automatics, the penetration was attempted. Initially the descent went very much as planned. Although vicious, the size of the granular domains in the turbulence was reasonably small, and several domains acting simultaneously on the hull were apt to cancel each other out to a minimum net effect on the ship's structure.

Ancor, nearly recumbent on his couch, was positioned so that he had a good view of the fleeting figures on the computer screens, but also relayed to him was the broader view of the external scanners which showed the images of the great aperture itself. As they swam below the amazing rim into the sea of turbulence, he could see nothing but the sheer walls rising on every side. Although the aperture was better than five thousand miles across, the magnificent electronic cameras gave him every detail of the smooth rock-face which led down to the cageworld cavity.

Then suddenly Ancor was swearing, punching the panic bulb strapped to his palm, and watching with fear and fascination as the great walls around them tumbled and broke swiftly as the impenetrable Exisfield which maintained the cavity and its approaches was withdrawn. Billions upon billions of tons of shell material, driven by the vast gravitational forces of the mammoth shell, strode into the aperture, and such were the pressures involved that the rock melted and flowed like water, transforming the whole scene into a vast cauldron of plunging fire.

Briefly he caught a glimpse of the cageworld far below, trapped into sudden immobility as its huge momentum was arrested by the surrounding shell crushing the cavity in which it had been spinning. The energy from the momentum was released as further heat, and suddenly the pitiful little world was cracking, crazing, slipping slowly into an awe-inspiring vortex of incandescent matter from which shot furious streamers a thousand miles in length. The cageworld and the material round the aperture enjoined to become one vast whirlpool of rotating, overheated matter which spiralled crazily deeper to form a funnel into which the *Shellback* seemed drawn as if by a magnet. A complex web of gravitational and electromagnetic forces gripped the little ship, spun it, and drew it inexorably down into the hellish maw.

Transfixed by the sight of their approach into this infernal, spinning pit, Ancor found he could do nothing. The *Shellback* had long been thrust into the emergency-flight mode, and he could hear the engines straining to lift the ship away. Such was the power of the forces which gripped them, however, that even the magnificent space-mode engines were unable to do more than slow their descent, and the greedy, furious tube of rotating fire drew them even deeper between its diabolical walls.

Their deliverance was a pure accident of chance and physics. When the shell-mass had crushed the cageworld, the atmosphere, the water, and all the volatiles on the world had been trapped, had merged and blended, melded by heat and pressure, and finally formed one vast pocket of white-hot gas still deep inside the plastic ferment of the vortex mass. Suddenly this broke through to the surface, and screamed for release towards the vacuum of Nepturan-space. As this cosmological belch took place, it encountered the struggling *Shellback* in its path, and swept the little ship along to throw it out of the well on a tide of incandescent gas. Once clear of the electromagnetic web which had entrapped it, the game little ship's engines were able precariously to lift it away to safety.

Nobody said anything for a long time. Cherry finally recovered control from the emergency-flight mode, and Ancor was busy checking out the integrity of the ship's hull and estimating the damage to his instruments. The others came out of their crash cocoons and stared with amazement at the bright whirlpool which still dominated the screens. Finally Cherry broke the silence.

"That was quite some performance, Maq!" he said plaintively. "I wonder what they'll do for an encore?"

CHAPTER TWELVE

Tri-Atomic

"EXPLAIN TO ME what happened," asked Sine.

"They took one hell of a risk withdrawing the Exis field which maintained that cavity. That has to be a measure of the concern with which they regard our coming."

"I don't see why you say they took a risk. Surely we were the ones at risk?"

"Let me put it this way, Sine. They deliberately switched off the Exis field, so that the shell moved in and crushed the cavity. Presumably they didn't want us to get through the interspace, and in theory it should have destroyed us altogether. But you can't stop a mass like a cageworld from rotating without a great deal of heat being evolved, to say nothing of the energy released by the sheer sudden movement of the shell's mass. They must have created shell-quakes which spread for millions of miles, and completely melted down the volcanic aperture leading to the outer surface."

"Is that important?"

"Vitally so. The net effect was a spinning vortex of molten rock with a hollow core. Now, what retains the atmosphere on the outer surface of the shell is the gravitational attraction of the shell-mass and the fact that the cageworld aperture is around a thousand miles high. Up there the atmosphere is so rare that leakage through the cageworld cavity is minimal."

"So?"

"Imagine their predicament if, after having melted down the aperture protrusion itself, that vortex tube had connected with both the inner and outer shell faces. Their entire atmosphere could have been drawn into the vacuum of Nepturan-space, and every person alive on the shell's outer surface would have died through lack of air."

"Do you think they missed that point?"

"I don't know. Perhaps they had another Exis plane ready to seal it off in case things did get out of hand. But I still see it as a hell of a risk to take, and the tremors in the shell must have done a lot of damage."

"You keep talking about 'they', Maq. Surely it's Zeus which controls the gross mechanics of the universe."

"Normally. But Zeus is a builder, not a destroyer. This is the same paradox we encountered with the eye—it could only have been done using Zeus' facilities, yet it was not Zeus which was using them. At a guess, Zeus is being usurped in some way."

"By the tyrant?"

"It's possible. Zeus is something like two thousand seven hundred million miles away, and therefore four hours out of touch with the latest news. And it's a further four hours before it can interfere if it doesn't like what it hears. If somebody could gain local control of Zeus' facilities at this distance, there would be virtually nothing Zeus could do about it. Any corrective action that it took would always be eight hours too late."

"What about Zeus' local executive centres?"

"On a shell this size, they could be equally ineffective. It would take thirteen hours for a radio signal to travel halfway round the shell. Unless Zeus has a great number of executive centres scattered round the shell, the chances are that the executives would be even more out of touch than is Zeus itself."

"So what are we going to do now, Maq?"

"We're going back to look for the cageworld aperture we couldn't find. I think the one we entered was set as a deliberate trap, and that's why it was made so easy to spot."

"You don't think they'll crash another one just to stop us getting through?"

"I doubt it. A shift of shell-mass like that must have done a hell of a lot of damage to the structure of the shell. From the number of Exis-plane generators there are dotted around, I'd say the structure was none too stable anyway. I don't think they'd dare risk another mass-shift, especially on this part of the equator."

"There is something that puzzles me, Maq. If these people— the tyrant or whoever—are really so powerful and so clever, why should they be so afraid of the few of us in the *Shellback*?"

"I suspect the answer is psychological. They must know they've got Zeus rattled, and they're probably waiting to see how a mammoth artificial intelligence like Zeus will attempt to solve its dilemma. Suddenly along comes the little *Shellback*, probably the first manned vessel ever to cross Nepturan-space. It shoots the hell out of one of their major space-scanning systems, and obviously intends to penetrate right through to the outer face. I suspect they confused us with Zeus' long-awaited means of retribution, and just to be on the safe side, they tried to get us first.''

"Seriously, would we stand any sort of chance against them?''

"Logic says no. But then remember one thing—Land-a originally put together this curious team of Cherry, you and I. We never could see the logic of it, but it's a mix of unlikely talents which has somehow survived every problem thrown at it. Cherry's genius with terrain holography, your proficiency in coquetry aided by elements of your aquatic ancestry, and my training in weaponry has taken us through to the centre of Solaria, and now brings us out to its fringes. Whatever it is we've got, it seems to work.''

"But that was before somebody started to confuse us with the hand of Zeus.''

"That's a point that has me worried. Basically we're here because Zeus influenced Land-a. Does Zeus confuse us with the hand of Zeus?''

Knowing the position of the ruined cageworld aperture with certainty, Ancor was able to calculate the location of the one he had previously been unable to find, and he gave this to Cherry as a course heading. It took them three days to reach the point, and when they did so it became obvious as to why it had not been easy to see before. An immense ridge in the uneven surface had completely swamped what should have been a thousand mile high volcano-like protrusion, and though the customary aperture was there it was visible only from directly above, and the machined "rim" was located nearly fifty miles below the surface.

They scanned for any signs of possible interference, and to establish the granular size of the turbulence. Finding nothing particularly unusual, the decision was taken to attempt the penetration. The heat leakage from the cageworld was only mild, indicating a cool climate yet one within the range of human tolerance, and all the instrument readings were so completely normal that had the world been in any other shell they would have gone to it without any hesitation. After their recent attempt to penetrate the Neptune shell, however, they all had to admit it was purely an act of faith which allowed them to accept that this aperture would not catastrophically implode around them.

The ship went down under automatic control, with the flight-emergency back-off system ready at the flash of an electron to pull them out again if any of the physical conditions they encountered did not tally within a few percent of the limits Ancor had pre-set into the computer. Having automated most of his observa-

71

tion chore, Ancor was free to lie in his couch and watch the progress of their passage on the scanner monitors. Apart from the distortion of the image caused by their progress through the turbulent regions, he found nothing of note, and was again able to savour the awe-inspiring sight of penetrating the great hole in the surface of the shell to find the "caged" little world which swum serenely in the cavity.

It was as they dropped below the turbulence and began to touch the fringes of the atmosphere that Ancor started to notice something out of the ordinary. Not considering what he had found to be sufficient cause to abort the penetration, he canceled the emergency-flight system and instructed Cherry to make the slowest possible descent through the atmosphere whilst he ran some instrumental checks. Soon he had his answer. Whilst both elemental nitrogen and oxygen were present in the atmosphere in approximately breathable proportions, the bulk of the oxygen was in the wrong molecular form. Instead of being the normal diatomic oxygen so essential to human life, this oxygen was mainly present as the poisonous, unbreathable triatomic form, and it was present in a lethal concentration.

"Level her off about two miles up, Cherry. I don't think we'll be going down."

"Trouble, Maq?"

"The atmosphere's loaded with ozone, which is a rather nasty substance if you get too much of it. I doubt if any vegetation could survive it, and higher life-forms are definitely out."

"I always thought ozone was good for you."

"Small traces of it are useful for freshening stale air and the like, but the amount that's down there would sterilise anything. It's a powerful oxidant, and its effect on tissues can be as bad as an overdose of radiation."

"Surely Zeus wouldn't go to the bother of building a cageworld and then deliberately give it a poisonous atmosphere?"

"It could just have been a slip in the specification. Or it could be something more. We can't see any of the local luminaries from here, but when we do I'll lay odds that they're operating with a spectrum well into the ultra-violet."

Hearing the change of engine note as Cherry brought the ship to hover, the others had come out of their crash cocoons and gone to the observation bay to see what this new world had to offer. Finding nothing but darkness below, Sine had opened up one of the visual scanners to probe the terrain, and was still doing so when Maq walked in.

"You're wasting your time, Sine. Nothing could live down there."

"I think you're wrong, Maq. Even from this height I'm pretty sure I can see trees and vegetation. And where they can live, so usually can more advanced forms of life."

"What you're seeing is an illusion. That's an ozone atmosphere down there. The air is poisonous, the water would make an excellent steriliser, and if any vegetable could survive, it would be completely inedible."

She looked up as she heard the thrusters re-start. "We aren't leaving so soon, are we?"

"No. I've asked Cherry to catch up with one of the local luminaries. They must be operating well into the ultra-violet band, and the question is why. The normal composition for a proto-star has been optimised to give the radiation bands most suited to the ecology. I'm wondering if these particular luminaries have been tampered with."

"Don't be silly! How could anyone tamper with a luminary?"

"Someone with access to Zeus' facilities could. The cageworld which got crushed was over-hot. This one looks as though it's being deliberately sterilised. Two rogue cageworlds on the route through to Hades could be something more than a coincidence."

"But an ozone atmosphere won't stop the *Shellback* going through."

"No. But then they'd no reason to expect the *Shellback*. They might, for instance, have been anticipating the arrival of an exospheric fleet, attempting to set up an armed base down there. Then an ozone atmosphere would be a very effective deterrant."

The search for the luminary was soon complete. Working towards the slight suggestion of a pale dawn, they quickly drew over the horizon and came in sight of a proto-star which shone with the most beautiful mercurial blue. Ancor watched the print-out of its radiation spectra with a thoughtful frown.

"Yes, it has been tampered with, and the radiation is sufficiently ionising to account for the ozone in the atmosphere. There are elements in it which should never be present in a luminary, and the concentration of some of the others has been altered. But it appears to have been done over a relatively long span of time, because some of those isotopes have pretty considerable half-lives."

"You were wrong, Maq!" called Sine Anura, who had still remained at the scanner. "There are people down there. Come and see!"

Still only half believing, Ancor did as he was bid. In the half-light of the blue dawn, a small group of individuals, naked, and with skins of a super-white hue, were trekking up a long pass on the sides of which some form of vegetation was now clearly visible. From the spears and hammer-like axes which the party carried, they were obviously members of some very primitive society, and the whole scene was like a snapshot out of the earliest dawn of man's own history.

"Well, I'll be damned!" said Ancor. "A natural adaptation, or one of Zeus' mutant strains? We shall probably never know. But the point is that they can live where we can't, such is the resourcefulness of the human gene."

"Can we go down and visit them, Maq? Please!"

"I don't think so, Sine. It would mean us wearing full spacesuits—which would scare the hell out of them. And the combination of ozone and strong ultra-violet light could actually damage the fabric of our suits. I think I'll let Cherry free to make a holo-record of this world from the air. It'll look marvellous in the archives, but I don't want to take any unnecessary risks obtaining it. I've a feeling our real trials are still to come."

CHAPTER THIRTEEN

The Arms of Zeus

IT WAS A truly amazing scene. Having exchanged chlorophyll for some alternative photo-synthesis chemical, all the vegetation, the grasses, the shrubs and the trees on this strange cageworld were completely white. Quite different types of life chemistry must have evolved too, since all the forms were unusual, and the predominant plant was like a broad-leaved fern which at least from the air appeared stiff like veins of diamond-iridescent silica. All in all it was reminiscent of a scene taken from the bottom of a sea, and the only things which were not bleach-white were the rocks and the sands, which nevertheless showed restricted hues under the nearly monochromatic radiation of the blue luminaries.

They saw a few more· of the strange white people, casual hunting groups, working co-operatively at catching some rather elusive prey. Men, women, and children, they could have been moulded of flexible white marble, and all were hairless and completely naked. They moved like living statues across the bland veld, but though their lips were occasionally seen to be moving it was impossible to tell if they had yet evolved a language. The *Shellback* hovered as silently and unobtrusively as it could, where possible taking advantage of rocky ledges to render its presence less obvious, and Cherry's magnificent long-range terrain hologram equipment brought back pictures of amazing detail and clarity. If they were ever able to return safely to their base, this record would rank highly in the archives of the Centre for Solarian Studies, and the fact that these beautiful people lived and thrived under an atmosphere which would have been fully lethal to normal human beings added to rather than detracted from this impressive holo-play.

Finally Cherry decided that he had expended sufficient holo tape, and that further running would be essentially a duplication. In that time they had travelled nearly halfway round the world, flown over grey mountain ranges and water-white seas, and nowhere encountered anything more civilised than a few nomadic tribes. Despite Sine's pleas that they go down to the surface and actually experience the environment for themselves, Ancor held firm, and having completed his instrumental surveys for the records, he directed Cherry to fly on to find the aperture which would lead out of the cageworld interspace and on to the outer surface of the Neptune shell under the region of space called Hades.

Soon the great arc of the rim showed clear upon their scopes, and they hovered beneath one edge of it for many hours, scanning it warily and knowing that this was possibly the most dangerous emergence they had ever made. The instruments told them of nothing that was visibly amiss: the turbulence, though seething, was fine-grained and no worse than they had encountered when they had entered the cageworld cavity from the inner side, and no space machines or other suspicious objects were in view. Tez opened up the automatic weapons panel and armed a selection of torpedoes in the weapons bay, then strapped himself behind a cannon in readiness. With Carli and Sine in the crash cocoons, and Cherry safely contained in his cockpit, Ancor returned to his safety couch from where he could watch his screens and monitors, and then gave the order to proceed. He had taken every precaution available to him, and the only thing left was to watch and hope.

The flight was completely under the control of the automatics, and planned to carry them at maximum practicable speed through the turbulence, then to continue straight up into Hades-space for at least a further thousand miles above the aperture's rim. Here control of the ship would revert to Cherry, and hopefully the speed of their emergence would have rendered them less likely to be detected by any observers who were not actually located on the rim itself. As a precaution against the possibility that an invisible Exis plane had been established across their path, Ancor sent an unarmed space torpedo ahead of their path and tracked it until he was satisfied it had run to its destination without hindrance, and in its wake the *Shellback* followed fast.

Ancor's first view was a sense of anti-climax. The turbulence, though seething-fierce, was no more of a problem than they had anticipated, and as they swept past the great rim it was easy to ascertain that nothing dangerous was located on its glassy surface. Then they were rocketing into Hades-space, gathering speed rapidly, and the breathtaking view of the shell's surface they received as they emerged from the top of the thousand mile high volcano-like protrusion receded swiftly as they doubled their height above the vast, sweeping lands below them.

They had reduced their velocity and Cherry had begun to level off, when some of the instruments began to go wild, and their messages flashed large upon the screen. Ancor unstrapped himself and said: "Trouble!" to Cherry over the intercom.

"What sort of trouble, Maq? I've nothing on my screens."

"We're being bombarded with a high level microwave radiation. Looks like a beamed source. I'll give you more details in a moment."

In the meantime Sine had emerged from her cocoon and was looking with some concern at the flashing entry on the computer screen.

"What's adrift, Maq?"

"We're the target for an extremely powerful radio beam. From its strength, I'd say it was a bulk-power broadcasting transmitter."

"Is it dangerous?"

"It would be, if the *Shellback* wasn't so well shielded. Thanks to the foresight of Land-a's designers, all it's doing at the moment is to heat up the hull. But if it hadn't been for the shield design we could already have been in serious trouble biologically. Let's not kid ourselves, it's designed to kill us. I've never seen so tight a beam held right through to the exosphere. It takes a rare piece of technology to achieve that. Tez, get that source lined up for a diffract-meson warhead."

"Plotting it now, Maq."

"What action do you want me to take?" asked Cherry.

"Angle the ship so that our heat-dump radiators are facing spacewards, then fly round in circles."

"Are you kidding?"

"Never at a time like this. I want to see how well they can track us. Anyway, I suspect they'll turn it off when they see it's not having the desired effect."

"Weapon ready," said Tez. "Want me to try and knock it out?"

"Yes, but not until they turn it off."

"I don't understand. What's the point of waiting?"

"To gain a psychological edge. First we make the point that their weapon doesn't appear to worry us. Then we knock it out violently just to teach them a lesson. In the last analysis, tactics may be the only advantage we have. We can't possibly continue a running fight, so we have to make the immediate point that we're untouchable. It's our only chance."

"It doesn't sound much of a chance to me," said Sine Anura.

"It isn't. But it does have something going for it. From the scale on which they've reacted so far, I'd say it was certain they regarded us as representing the hand of Zeus. After all, what else is there in Solaria of which to be afraid? So let's adopt the mantle while it suits us: difficult to destroy and terrible in revenge."

"It seems all wrong to me that our first act on reaching the outer face of a new shell is to drop a diffract-meson warhead on it."

"I don't share your conscience, Sine. This is the second time they've tried to kill us without warning. Hostile, unprovoked attacks using mammoth technological resources. That we've survived at all is partly due to chance and partly due to Land-a's forethought. Could you expect me to continue to turn the other cheek?"

Ancor's expectation that the beam would shortly be withdrawn was not confirmed. As the hours dragged past it continued to hurl its vast energy into space, and after a few initial blunders it began to track the circling *Shellback* quite successfully. Ancor observed this with a deepening frown. Although the shielding in the ship attenuated the main bulk of the radiation, an inevitable small percentage did get through, and its effects would grow cumulative with time. Furthermore, the great static charges which were building up on the *Shellback*'s hull were interfering with a lot of his other instruments, and he had been forced to cease any attempts to use the intervening time to scan the shell itself.

Maq was reasonably confident that his diffract-meson weapon, put down at the point from which the beam originated, would solve the problem. The timing, however, was critical. If he knocked out the beam now, it could be interpreted that they had reached the limits of their tolerance. This was nearly true, but it was not a factor Ancor wished to expose. Equally, if they merely headed out into Hades-space they could reach a point where the beam could do them no possible harm, but again this was an admission of weakness. What he most needed was a way to break the dangerous impasse without losing stature, but at this point he had rejected all his notions on how this could be done.

Curiously, the impasse was broken for him, and in a way he could not possibly have imagined. With most of the ship's external monitors out of action due to the static charge, they had no prior warning of the happening, and the first they knew was when a sudden blinding glare of light plunged across the sky and hurtled towards the surface like an avenging thunderbolt. Immediately the radiation from the beam ceased, and Ancor yelled to Tez to stand by to fire the diffract-meson warhead, whilst he tried to find out what had taken place. The visual sensors, which had been unaffected by the static, told of something incredible. The beam's point of origin, which was intended to be the target for their own weapon, was already the centrepoint of a vast flare so broad and intense that it was perfectly visible from their position in space better than two thousand miles away. Like a miniature sun, it hung on the shell's surface like a ball of incandescent gold, and the heat sensors on the ship ran high with the intensity of its outpourings.

Swiftly Ancor bled the static from the *Shellback*'s hull by discharging ionised sodium into space, and brought the rest of his instruments back into use.

"What the hell is that?" asked Tez. "Did their powerplant blow up?"

Ancor was watching the screens as they rapidly filled with figures.

"Far too much energy for a powerplant, and anyway it came down out of the sky. It's more in the nature of a small protostar."

"A proto-star? How could that be?"

Ancor turned from the computer and began to operate the scanners, which were just clearing from the charge of static. After a while he grunted.

"That could be our answer, Tez. Way out there in Hades-space—a group of Zeus' spacekeepers."

"They're the things which fuel the luminaries?"

"They are, and at a guess they manufactured a small luminary out of the fissile dust and gas fuel, then set it on a course which intercepted with the shell."

"Which for us was a very lucky accident."

"I doubt if it was an accident. The placement is too precise. I think they deliberately targeted it on the beam projector."

"But why?"

Ignoring the projector, Ancor was working something out in his head. "I think I have it, Tez. One of Zeus' local executive centres must have let Zeus know what was going on, and Zeus ordered the beam installation to be destroyed. Figuring it from the time it would have taken for the message to reach Zeus and an instruction to be received back and implemented, it works out about right. Where the tyrant, or whoever, made his mistake was not so much in attacking us as in continuing the attack for too long."

"It's a hell of a drastic way to destroy a beam projector—dropping a luminary on it."

"Perhaps its symptomatic of the size of the problem, Tez. Serious ills call for drastic remedies. I doubt if we'll get such impressive assistance a second time, but the implications are damned interesting. Not only do the people of Neptune shell regard us as the hand of Zeus, but it would appear even Zeus itself thinks the same thing. Somehow we've been co-opted.''

With all their instruments now back in operation, they had an impressive view of the fireball as it gradually dwindled and died. It appeared to have been a short-lived luminary of limited mass, and it finally disappeared completely as its plasma became spent and dissipated. However, the ugly scar it left on the surface of the shell would probably remain a permanent feature. Thousands of square miles of the surface would have been sterilised by the heat and radiation, and the great glazed bowl formed at its point of contact would be now of rock so deeply heated that it might take centuries to cool.

CHAPTER FOURTEEN

The Bridge

WITH THEIR RECENT danger so dramatically removed and their instruments returned to normal, they now had the chance to examine their situation. At two thousand miles above the surface even the scanners were unable to resolve the finer details of the surface, and the variegated picture below them was a mere random patchwork of seas and land-masses, which blended indistinctly towards the great horizon of the shell. It was a mind-stretching exercise to consider that some of those small patches of blue were in reality great and raging oceans a thousand miles across, and some of the minute brows were mountain ranges so high and vast that a man might spend a lifetime attempting to climb them and never once succeed.

Ancor's first interest was in attempting to establish whether they were liable to another attack from any source. He could find no evidence of any further radiation beams, and the skies were completely clear, with no sign of exospheric or even atmospheric craft being used. There was always the possibility that they were in the target sights of some missile projector, but even at a minute fraction of that range the *Shellback*'s equipment could detect and destroy an approaching missile, so this was no particular problem. He could, in fact, find nothing at all to justify further caution, but the message of the crushed cageworld and the level of technology behind the space-eye, the altered luminaries, and the powerful radio beam made him trebly careful before he authorised Cherry to begin a cautious descent.

From the height of a thousand miles the scanners should have been able to start imaging patterns characteristic of the way the shell population utilised the terrain: whether they built their cities beneath the fields, or whether they concentrated their numbers into vast conurbations so as to leave as much space as possible for the growing of food. Even as the *Shellback* fell well below this height, however, neither of these patterns emerged, and they were forced to the conclusion that the citizens of the Neptune shell must have adopted a radically new approach to the problem of feeding and housing an ever-increasing multitude. Assuming the shell to be populated to no more than the Solarian target-figure of ten thousand people to the square mile, there should be five hundred thousand million million million people on the shell, and any scheme which could conceal them so effectively from the prying eye of the scanner was fully worth investigating.

There was another peculiarity which Ancor noticed when he began to monitor the radio waveband. There were transmissions in plenty, but all of it apparently in crowded code-message form, with not a single channel seemingly being used for voice or music. It was quite possible that both speech and music were being transmitted in some digital-encoded form, but when Ancor ran a computing exercise on some sample transmissions he was unable to discover what special codes might be being used, and was forced to the conclusion that those he had tried to analyse were simply conversations between machines.

As they approached the bottom of the exosphere, a mere two hundred miles above the surface, they expected to be challenged and possibly even intercepted, and all their anti-missile and defence mechanisms were fully alert against the possibility of sudden attack. No action of any kind was forthcoming, however, and had it not been for their earlier encounter with the micro-wave beam they would have sworn their presence had not even been detected. Even more strangely, the patterns of land utilisation were still not appearing on the screens, and this was a mystery which remained even when, at the height of one bare mile above the surface, Ancor called for Cherry to level off and hover.

Sine Anura joined Maq in the observation bay, and together they began to examine the area with optical telescopes. Here the shell surface had been terraformed to give broadly-rolling pasture land, lightly wooded, with gentle slopes and an engaging river which meandered idly between uncaring banks. After their long confinement in the crowded confines of the *Shellback*, the place looked like Paradise, but their appraisal was of more than pastoral interest, because they were still trying to discover how the people were integrated into the scheme.

The possibility of an underground community was not forgotten. One other shell in the Solarian system had a population which lived entirely underground and eschewed the surface. That shell, however, was a special case, and there were very good reasons behind the arrangement. On the Neptune shell these reasons did not appear to apply, and nothing about the tranquil scene gave any clues as to where the population was or why it was so hard to find. Of course, many major shells still had occasional under-populated or unpopulated parts, but the chance of arriving at one of these by accident was statistically very slight.

Sine expressed what Ancor had already decided but been unable to believe with conviction.

"There's nobody down there, Maq! Nobody at all."

"I guessed it a while ago, Sine. But I just wanted to see it with my own eyes. During our descent we've intensively scanned a strip of terrain over twenty-seven thousand miles in length, and never seen the suggestion of a city. And something else hasn't shown up either—crops. Not a single corn-belt, not a field even. If there is a population here it must be very assured of food supply to waste so much arable land."

"Do you think any people do live here?"

"Somebody fired that beam at us, that's for sure. No, I guess they're on some other part of the shell which we haven't seen yet. What we've come across may be some sort of national park or nature reserve, but it's curiously fortunate that we happened to run across it on first contact."

"What's curiously fortunate about it, Maq?"

"Do you realise how many months we've been cooped up in this damn machine? We all need a holiday, Sine. I've a few more instrument checks to carry out, but if I'm satisfied, then we'll drop right down there and do just nothing at all for a while."

She was delighted. "Oh Maq! Could we?"

"I see nothing against it. Of course we'll have to take turns to man the *Shellback*'s monitors to make sure nothing sneaks up on us, but from a reasonably high point we can put out a radar scan which should give us ample warning of the approach of anything short of a ballistic missile."

A frown of uncertainty creased the green attractiveness of her brow.

"This isn't like you, Maq. We came all this way to find out about the tyrant, and you propose to start the quest by putting your feet up. It's human, humane and rational, but it isn't Maq Ancor's style. You've something else in mind."

He caught her under the chin and kissed her.

"Of course I have, Sine! It's a question of logistics. Do you know that if you took a strato-plane which did a thousand miles an hour, it would take you two thousand years to fly right round the Neptune shell? Have we any chance of finding the tyrant just by flying round looking for him? The answer is no. The only way we'll ever get a clue about what is going on here is to stay in one place and advertise our presence. They will have to come to us. Life is too short for any other approach to work."

"And what if they don't come?"

"I think they will. They saw us coming, tried to prevent us getting here, and tried to destroy us once we'd arrived. That's not actually a model of disinterestedness. So we watch and wait. And in the meantime we have a holiday."

The *Shellback* landed on the crest of a mild hill which happened to be the highest feature in the district. It was a fortunate location, because it also closely overlooked a stretch of the river, and could have been chosen for the excellence of its scenic views alone. On the far horizon on one side of them was a barely-visible range of snow-capped mountains, whilst on the other side the distance blended straight into the vagueness of the sky. The terrain-scanning radar could cover all of the area except patches of dead ground behind the ridges for at least a hundred-mile radius, and the sky-watching radar could probe right to the upper fringes of the exosphere. Not even a light aircraft could have entered the range without detection, and any ground-based approach should be spotted hours before it could arrive.

The last thing Ancor did was to arrange a deception. On another hill some three miles distant he set up a powerful radio beacon, broadcasting the ship's call signature. The final move he left to Cherry, who went out with Tez and made a terrain hologram of a thickly wooded copse nearby. When the holo-projectors were brought out from the pod and the tape re-run, the copse marvellously appeared to grow anew on the hill-top, completely camouflaging the *Shellback*, and so realistic was the reproduction that even the birds tried resting on the branches and then flew away amazed and perturbed at its insubstantiality.

With this electronic "bower" as their base, they then relaxed, only one of them at a time being concerned with attending to the ship's monitors. After the wearisome months of confinement in the *Shellback*'s crowded bays, they could scarcely have wished for a better spot to unwind. The grassy banks were succulent and green, and the air had a pleasing mildness which was a balm to lungs grown tired of constantly recycled air. Although they all carried arms in case they should meet with something unexpected and dangerous, they encountered no wildlife which was not timidly elusive, and soon they gained confidence and began to range from their base as far as their feet would carry them. Sine Anura, with an inbuilt longing for the aquatic habitat of some of her Engelian ancestors, made full use of the river, frequently returning with fresh, edible fish, which made a very welcome change from their normal diet of reconstituted concentrates.

Indeed, it was Sine who discovered the bridge. Apart from the microwave beam they had encountered when first arriving, the bridge was the first actual indication they had had that there were indeed people on the Neptune shell. Her speed in the water, even against the sluggish current, was considerably greater than her normal speed on land, and she had taken to swimming twenty or thirty miles downstream just for the exercise. It was on her first trip upstream that she came across the bridge, nearly a four-hour walk when she led Ancor to it.

As a structure, the bridge was not exceptional. Three columns of hewn granite blocks supported a carefully arched structure again of massive granite, and the whole had an impressive air of rustic age and durability. The stony surface of its deck gave way at either end simply to grassy slopes where no true tracks had formed, suggesting that the bridge itself was very little used. Further examination yielded no clues as to its builders or intended users, and they were about to dismiss it as a charming curiosity when Ancor, rising from his knees where he had been examining the stones, looked up suddenly and saw the trail in the grass which was marked only by the way the leaves had been slightly flattened by something which had passed across the bridge quite recently.

Experimentally he walked through a patch of grass, and then examined the track he had made. It was quite different. Whatever had crossed the bridge had not actually touched the ground beneath, and the leaves had been blown aside rather than parted by a wheel or a foot. Something moderately small, possibly in the nature of a one or two-man hover vehicle, had come this way whilst they had been walking along the meandering river bank, and looking at the grass from a low angle it was possible to see that the track actually curved towards the position of the little ship and had taken a route which was shorter than their own path along the curve of the river.

Ancor's hand flew to the radio transceiver at his belt and he began calling the ship urgently, but at no time, even whilst running, could he get a reply.

CHAPTER FIFTEEN

Carim Carim

EVEN THOUGH THE ship was sitting on the highest point in the locality, the *Shellback*'s terrain-scanning radar had needed to be trimmed to avoid unwanted reflections from tree-tops and other nearby objects, and the computer was using its discretion in removing from the scan display features arising locally and below a critical pre-set angle. It was for this reason that Tez, who was on monitoring duty at the time, completely missed the coming of the hover-truck until it was actually visible through the window of the observation bay. The vehicle had come virtually silently along the low ground of the river-valley, and at a speed not much more than twice that of a walking man, and had therefore been discounted by the equipment, which was looking for faster and more distant objects.

Tez's first reaction on seeing the vehicle so close, was one of shock. The swiftly rotating dishes on the 'tower' behind the single occupant immediately suggested radio-detection equipment, and it forcibly occurred to Tez that Maq's radio beacon had been deliberately placed at a distance from the *Shellback* in order to keep concealed the whereabouts of the ship itself. Yet the ship was running its radar transmitters, and therefore broadcasting its position. Putting the implications together with a rare flash of insight, Tez immediately killed the radar and waited with stilled breath to see if it had already been pinpointed. Because of the necessity to maintain radio silence he was additionally unable to contact Maq or Cherry and Carli, who had taken cameras and gone to photograph wildlife.

Obviously unaware of the actual location of the *Shellback* nestling in its holo-image camouflage, the hover-truck pulled out into the open field, then stopped uncertainly, as if suddenly missing the radar transmissions but still being aware of the beacon on the farther hill. For five minutes the occupant, a lean, tanned individual clad in a light-grey tunic suit and sporting a bright-red pillbox hat, sat and studied the instruments before him, whilst Tez sat behind one of the *Shellback*'s cannons and wondered if there was some critical point at which he ought to open fire. The object of Maq's exercise was to establish communication with the population, but this obviously had to be on Maq's own terms, and achieved without risk to the *Shellback*. There was a device on the front of the hover-truck which looked to Tez rather like a weapon, and he resolved that if this was turned in the direction of the ship he would fire first rather than take the risk that the *Shellback* might be damaged.

Finally the hover-truck moved off in the direction of the beacon and Tez breathed a sigh of relief at this temporary respite from his dilemma. Shortly after the truck had disappeared from view behind some trees, Cherry and Carli came scrambling breathlessly to the ship, having hidden when the vehicle had unexpectedly come along. With forethought, Cherry had managed to get some photographs of the truck, and his goatee beard waggled with nervousness as they examined them.

"We have to tell Maq immediately."

"We daren't," said Tez. "With that radio thing out there we daren't risk transmitting. The only thing we can do is wait till he comes back."

"I could go and look for him," volunteered Carli.

"If you knew just where to look. He went up-river with Sine along the bank, but they could easily come back cross-country. Then we'd lose track of you, too. No, better we all stay. At least we're safe in the *Shellback*."

The sudden cessation of noise from one of the monitoring speakers told them that the hover-truck had reached the beacon and put it out of action. Whether this had been achieved by switching or by some more violent method was not apparent, but the new silence brought home to the three in the *Shellback* how completely dependent they were on Maq and Sine Anura for initiative in defensive and offensive action. Soon Carli gripped Tez's arm.

"It's coming back. See, it's stopped. It knows that something's here."

"We were running the radars earlier," said Tez. "He must be wondering where that came from."

"Do you think he'll see us?"

"If he were an expert on holo-projection he'd be able to see this terrain image wasn't the real thing. If he didn't know where to look for interference fringes, he'd never spot it.''

The lean man from the hover-truck had detached the device from the front of his vehicle, and was walking in their general direction. It was obvious from his exact path that he still did not know of the ship's precise location, but from the thoughtful look on his tanned face it was probable that he suspected that something suspicious lay in the area. Tez climbed back behind the cannon and kept the fellow aligned in his sights, but his fingers were well clear of the firing button.

The stranger began to climb the hill, then cut a diagonal path across it, missing the insubstantial fringes of the holo-image by no more than a few feet. Finally he sat down at a point overlooking the river, as if he needed time to think through the mystery of a space-vehicle which had to be there yet which he could not find. Only twenty yards away, the crew of the *Shellback* moved very cautiously indeed lest some slight sound should arouse the fellow's suspicions, and thus they waited for Maq to arrive to break the impasse.

Then the man rose suddenly and looked sharply along the river bank, raising the device which he had brought with him as though it were a gun. Ancor, breathless with running, burst through a patch of bushes into clear view, and froze into immobility as he saw the stranger and the instrument which was trained upon him.

The stranger's action was quite deliberate. Keeping his weapon levelled, he walked slowly towards the statuesque Ancor, and as he walked, his left hand was tuning some control on the instrument, which he held with his right hand, as though adjusting the device for maximum effort over an ever-decreasing range. Thirty feet away from Ancor he halted and began to take a careful two-handed sighting. Tez brought the cannon round, and was just screwing up his determination to fire when Carli let out a little squeal of excitement. Sine Anura, like a leaping dolphin, had catapulted herself out of the river slightly behind the man, and with a few swift strides she was upon him. It was doubtful if he even registered her approach before her fingers brushed his temples and he dropped like a stone at her feet.

''Is he dead?'' asked Carli, when they all met on the bank.

Ancor had been bent over the body, examining it.

''No, but he will be if we don't move fast. Get the medical float here quickly, Tez. Here, Sine, help me apply artificial respiration.''

Tez sped quickly on his errand, and soon the automated equipment on the float had taken over the urgent work of artificial respiration and resuscitation. Leaving Sine Anura to supervise the man's revival, Ancor then heard a quick summary of the preceding events from Tez, and together they went to where the hover-truck stood motionless in the grass. Even a quick look told them it was a machine of the highest sophistication, and when Ancor had finished his examination he shook his head with an appreciation at the tantalisingly high level of technology which it represented. For all its marvels, the *Shellback* was a clumsy and pedestrian mechanism by comparison.

On their way back to the ship Maq also began to study the weapon-like device which he had picked up after the stranger had fallen to Sine's electric fingers. The 'gun' was shaped like nothing he had ever seen before, and he pointed it at a group of bushes and squeezed the trigger to see what would happen. Something reacted in the instrument, but there was no apparent effect whatever on the bushes, except that a small bird fell from a branch to the ground. He picked the tiny creature up and examined it and decided it was still living. He placed it gently on the ground again and watched, and shortly it revived, strutted drunkenly for a moment or two, then finally flew away apparently none the worse for its experience.

"I think this is some sort of stun weapon," he said to Tez. "Designed to render people unconscious, but not necessarily to kill."

"He may not have come out to kill us, then?"

"I think it's unlikely that he did, since he came alone and made no attempt at concealment. I think he came merely to find out what was going on."

"He was definitely looking for the *Shellback*, and was puzzled when he couldn't find it."

"That's interesting, because he might have been sent specifically to make contact with us—in which case we misjudged his motives rather sadly. Let's go and see if he's recovered yet."

By the time they returned, the medical float had been drawn up near the *Shellback* amidst the insubstantial greenery of the holo-image, and the stranger was beginning to stir. Finally he opened his eyes and stared uncomprehendingly at the curious scene of the ugly little ship from which apparently sprouted living branches and tree-trunks. He reached out a hand and tested an apparent branch which had visual but no physical existence, and his lips became pursed in a rueful smile. Then he turned his head round to where Ancor and the attractively green Sine Anura were watching curiously.

"Are you shadows and illusions too?" he asked. In the circumstances, his composure was remarkable.

"No, we are only too real," Ancor assured him, keeping a handgun pointed very deliberately towards the fellow's chest. "Now tell me who you are, and what purpose brings you to this place."

The stranger smiled his rueful smile again. "I should be asking you that. My name is Carim Carim, and I live here. In fact, all these lands you see around are mine. And now you know my name, let me guess at yours." He was looking with something approaching wonder at the green shininess of the girl. "You would be Maq Ancor, and this delightful apparition can only be Sine Anura, from Engelian stock unless I miss my guess."

Ancor's hand jerked his weapon up rapidly. "How could you possibly know our names?"

"Your names were easy to establish. What I don't know is the purpose of your journey."

"We're an expeditionary party from the Centre for Solarian Studies," said Ancor. He was carefully watching to see what sort of reaction the statement produced.

"An interesting fiction," said Carim Carim, turning the statement aside. "But then I wonder if you know the truth yourselves."

"Why should you think it a fiction?"

"Because we've known for a long time that somebody would be sent, and on whose behalf."

"How did you know?"

Carim Carim smiled easily. "Look, Maq Ancor, there is much we could discuss. I am willing to answer your questions, but not here on my back with a gun at my chest. I invite all of you to be guests at my household. There we shall talk."

Ancor remained unmoved.

"Since we arrived at this shell there have been two attempts to kill us. If we come with you, what guarantees our safety?"

"You have my word on it. Earlier we were not convinced that you could call on the services of so powerful a protector. Now we no longer doubt it. I dare challenge many things in life, but Zeus isn't one of them."

"Lead the way on your vehicle," said Ancor. "And we will follow in our ship. But remember we have plenty of weapons, and at the slightest sign of treachery we will use them. Do you understand?"

"You needn't worry. I think on this whole shell we have not

90

one device which was specifically designed to kill a man. We have no need for such things."

"Treachery needs no weapons," said Ancor. "Sometimes merely a thought is sufficient."

Carim Carim smiled fleetingly. "And what then would you do? Drop another sun on me?"

CHAPTER SIXTEEN

Seonasere

ON MINIMUM THRUST the little ship rose delicately to no more than fifty feet, where it hovered to let Carim Carim get under way with his ground vehicle. This was the shellman's first opportunity to view the blocked ugliness of the *Shellback* in its entirety, shorn of the holo-image which had hidden it on the hill, and he stood with his hands on his hips in open ground and watched as it ascended, a smile of critical interest on his face. When it had stopped rising and was clearly waiting for him, he waved cheerfully, then ran to start his hover-truck.

"And what has my old lion found to worry him now?" asked Sine Anura, coming into the observation bay where Ancor was looking pensively down at their guide, whose bright red hat was an easily identifiable patch of colour against the greens and browns of the surrounding landscape.

Ancor shook his head, and the great mane of red hair flared round his collar like a beast of the jungle preparing itself for action.

"Something about all this is incredibly wrong, Sine. Carim Carim's reactions don't ring true at all. He's too composed, too well balanced."

"He came as an ambassador, Maq. Aren't ambassadors supposed to be like that?"

"Sine, he asked if we were prepared to drop another sun on him. How would you approach the occupants of a strange craft from another shell who appeared to have access to a trick like that?"

"Very cautiously indeed,"

"Yet Carim Carim rides out with a smile on his face, and blithely invites us home to tea. And was too nice to mention that a few minutes earlier you'd damn nigh killed him."

"I begin to see what you mean. It isn't natural. What approach do we take to this one, Maq?"

"I think you've aroused his interest, Sine. Make a play for him. See if you can find out what sort of creature he is."

"I think I might enjoy that." Sine licked her lips mischievously. "And what will you be doing while I'm working?"

"Trying to crack their communications codes. If our friend is right that they don't need weapons on the Neptune shell, then why the hell should their messages be so tightly cyphered? What are they hiding, and from whom?"

Carim Carim's progress on the hover-truck was leisurely to say the least. He seldom exceeded fifteen miles an hour, and turned frequently to wave cheerfully up at the ship which followed a mere fifty feet above. Such expansive gestures were no problem for him, because he was using some form of "hands-off" control for his vehicle, which meant that when he wasn't waving he was able to ride easily with his arms folded, enjoying the slow passing of the landscape.

About an hour later they passed over the bridge across the river, and Carim Carim set a straight course across slowly rising ground that led them finally to another valley where the meandering river had again turned upon itself. Here there were cultivated fields, though not the massive acreages of intensive cultivation they were accustomed to see—this was more in the nature of a home-farm, and obviously designed to supply the needs of a very limited number. There were a few workers in the fields, and Ancor immediately turned a telescope upon them, then grunted in surprise.

"Robots, Sine. In a mimic humanoid form. This place is crazy! The bulk of Solaria is choking to death with a surfeit of human beings, and here they're having to employ robot labour because they've apparently not enough people to do the work."

"So what does happen to all the emigrants who come out on the spoke shuttles?"

"We shan't really know that until we get to one of the terminals, though we may get some ideas from happy little Carim Carim there. What strikes me is that not only is the Neptune shell grossly underpopulated, but this appears to be deliberate. Otherwise it would have paid to establish a small farming community here just to keep the fields tended. In no way does it make economic sense to employ sophisticated robots when you have ample human labour available."

"Is this the sort of thing that has Zeus worried, do you think?"

"From the resources which went into the building of this

shell, and the size of it, it should be carrying a minimum average population of around ten thousand people to the square mile. But from what we've seen so far, it's more likely they've ten thousand square miles per person here. That's a neat little inversion, if you can get away with it. And the fact that they are getting away with it suggests that Carim Carim and his ilk have a lot more going for them than appears on the surface. No wonder Zeus is going crazy about it. We have to be careful, Sine. I think we're heading into big trouble.''

Around one last bend in the river Carim Carim's destination came into view. They had travelled at their slow pace for ninety miles, and the journey had taken them nearly six hours, but now the frustrations with the slowness of the trip were washed suddenly away by the sight of Carim Carim's household nestling against the side of the hill. It was almost a village of sturdy, round, white houses, spiralled like conch shells, with attractive little windows which blended into the opalescence of the skilfully-fluted walls. Here and there were larger buildings of similar design, but ornamented with minarets and twisted spires, made marvellous with imaginative balconies, and sporting unexpected flying buttresses which seemed to have no purpose except that they unified the design. The whole establishment was a palace fit for a king of kings, and Carim Carim was expansively waving them to descend on to a little white courtyard near the centre of the complex, and from the smile on his face, he was very pleased with himself indeed.

Ancor watched their descent thoughtfully. "No roads," he said, "no airstrips, and no landing pads. Unless they have helicopters and land in open fields, there's no way for Carim Carim and his crew to ever leave here. If there was a town within a thousand miles, we'd surely have seen it, so hovertrucks are out as a means of going places. This gets odder by the minute. You're all to carry arms, and I want a grav-lock on the ship so that nobody can enter or move it. Above all, stay alert.''

"What are we watching out for?" asked Tez.

"For whatever it is that gives our host such a territorial advantage over the rest of humanity. Anything which might give us a clue about the tyrant.''

Carim Carim met them in the splendid hall of one of the larger buildings. The luxury of the interior fully matched the playful extravagance of the exterior: the drapes and paintings and ornaments were nearly overwhelming with their rich and imaginative designs, and even the artistry of their placement suggested the work of a rare genius.

"Welcome to Seonasere! My household is at your service.

Rooms have been prepared for you, and the robots will fetch you anything you need."

"You indeed have an impressive place," said Ancor. "How many people live here?"

"People?" A slight frown crossed Carim Carim's face, and then he suddenly smiled again. "There is only me. I have plenty of robots. What should I want with people?"

"Something called human companionship?" asked Ancor.

"Ah, I knew it! A different philosophy. We must talk about it. I take it you're of the opinion that you cannot have a meaningful relationship with a machine?"

"Something like that."

"What a delightfully quaint idea! I shall look forward to converting you. But food is being prepared, and you will doubtless wish to bathe and rest before eating. Come, I will have robots show you to your rooms."

As they followed their mechanical guide up the ornate stairs and along the draped and alcoved corridors, Ancor found himself mentally summing the robot which strode so deliberately ahead. Of roughly human proportions but slimmer, the creature had a degree of muscle co-ordination which easily rivalled Ancor's own. No pretence had been made to give it human facial features, and its curved metal-looking visage was probably transparent to whatever radiation bands it was employing for its internal sensors. Its blued body was an impressive piece of fine engineering, seemingly composed of hardened alloy steel, yet such was the subtlety of its design that its limbs moved as though composed of living flesh, and the dexterity of its fingers was amazing. Ancor, trying to estimate its strength and reaction speed, came to the conclusion that if it came to unarmed combat he would himself certainly be the loser. His fingers involuntarily curled around the butt of his sidearm. He was not happy living in close proximity to a creature potentially more deadly than himself.

In the over-hot and darkened cell in Bryhn on the Mars shell, the man who was more machine than man steadied his carriage again before the awful terminal. Under the light of the solitary lamp the spines of the thousand-way connector seemed to blend to a single golden focal point which called with a near-hypnotic attraction. Land-a's face was a mask of sweat and tension, and the perspiration draining down his neck could literally have been wrung from the cloth of his collar and cravat. Without exception his life-support monitors were flashing brightly red, signalling that the essential synchronisation of his artificial body functions

was on the verge of breakdown. Whilst he retained consciousness he still had the choice of whether to use the terminal and
suffer the DREAMS and live, or whether to take the easy way
out and stay where he was and die. If he could only hold out
until the onset of the coma, the agony of the decision would
forever be lifted from him.

But as ever before, when the black bat of approaching death
swooped upon him, his love of life proved stronger than his fear
of the dreaded empathy. It was a subconscious rather than a
conscious resolve which initiated the movement of his carriage
towards the terminal post, and he had afterwards no actual
knowledge of fishing for the mating coupling; but somehow it
was drawn out of its niche, and the self-aligning surfaces were
slammed together with a noise which even his ears did not
register. And suddenly he was swamped by

DREAMS!!

Had his body been shattered by some inner explosion, the
effect could not have been more dramatic. He felt he was being
wrenched apart, disemboweled, atomised, dissipated by strange
winds. Then suddenly he became an isolated consciousness free-
floating in space. His mind seemed literally millions of miles
from his body, and he was an insubstantial spectator trying to
come to terms with an impression of a small sun falling from
space and plunging destructively at the surface of a shell. Surrounding that dreadful fall was a sensation of savage fury so
powerful and virulent that the only description which seemed apt
was a terrifying cosmic anger. It was a dreadful and violent tide
of emotion which coursed through every molecule of Land-a's
bio-mechanical composite body and left him gasping, drained
and helpless.

Through the empathy, he was sharing the wrath of Zeus . . .

The bright barb of anger represented by the fallen sun was
replaced then by tides of darkness and brooding apprehension.
This was a return to the black dreams, the colossal insecurities,
the feeling of great things inexorably getting beyond control, a
sense of utter helplessness in the face of the tyrant's stranglehold.

The face of the tyrant . . .

Although the tube in which he lived was locked rigidly on its
carriage, Land-a felt himself swaying, dizzied suddenly by the
vertiginous sensation of a fall. Suddenly he was looking at the
face of the tyrant, and struggling to understand what it was he
was being shown. Again and again he hurled his intellect against
the challenge, and each time it bounced off the concept like a

ball bouncing off a concrete wall. Then came a breakthrough in understanding, and the shattering comprehension was such that the dark and over-heated cell was filled with one great, unbidden cry of anguish.

Another shift in perspective, this time tinged with shades of hope, and a cameo, a portrait almost, of a face he actually knew. A face so complex with lines and puckers that it had the compelling ugliness of a jungle animal—a lion with a ruffled mane, a destroyer with a human heart. Viewed through what unknown lenses, the picture was unmistakable. Maq Ancor was stalking in the tyrant's realms, and shading him like a guardian angel was the terrible wrath of Zeus.

CHAPTER SEVENTEEN

Withdrawal

ANCOR AND SINE were given adjoining rooms, with an interconnecting doorway between. The rooms were large and luxurious, and Ancor sensed that when guests were entertained in the household it was probably a rare occasion and one which might continue for an extended period of time. This appeared to agree with the fact that there were no roads in the area. People so seldom came and went that roads were not essential.

Whilst he bathed, Ancor observed that a robot came and removed his travel-soiled clothing. He mentally saluted Carim Carim's household arrangements, expecting the garments to be swiftly returned, cleaned and pressed. The robot did not come back, however, and soon, looking for something with which to cover his nakedness, Ancor started to pry through the cupboards. He found plenty of clothing, all of it completely new. It was when he started to dress that the big shock came: by what he could only consider a coincidence, every single garment was a perfect fit, and even his concealed weapons pockets had been neatly sewn in place.

Whilst he was still pondering on this curious fact, Sine Anura came in through the connecting door, stunningly arrayed in a new dress which appeared to be made of flowing gold. The style and fit were sheer perfection. To crown the image, a tiara rich with dazzling jewels adorned her head, and on her arms were bangles each in value worth more than Ancor expected to earn in a lifetime.

"I think the room service here is rather good," she said.

"You don't know how good, Sine," said Ancor. "When was the last time you were fitted for a dress?"

"Just before we left on this trip. In the Liss-mal in Zapoketa on Saturn shell. Why?"

"Doesn't that feel like the same fitting?"

She frowned thoughtfully. "Yes, it does, rather. What are you driving at, Maq?"

"The shoes I found even feel as though they were made on my personal last. So the mystery deepens. Not only did Carim Carim know our names, but he also knows everything about us, right down to the fit of our clothes."

"It's not possible."

"I think it might be. Right throughout Solaria there's a vast web of information exchange operated by Zeus for the purpose of regulating the universe and controlling the population head-counts. Part of that system is the Solarian Identifile, which keeps track of everyone from the day they're born to the day they die. Now, Identifile identification is always positive. It never makes a mistake. That could only be achieved if a whole barrow-load of trivia about each of us was recorded alongside the more obvious data. I think somehow Carim Carim has gained access to our complete Identifile records."

"Why the hell should they bother?"

"Probably because they think Zeus has sent us, and that the more they know about us the more chance they have to negate our advantages. I think these clothes were provided as a bit of bravado, to let us know they're smarter than we think. But the robots are more serious. I wouldn't care to tackle one unarmed, and if they're made of the alloy I think they are, I would be lucky to stop one with a high-explosive pellet. Nor, my pet, would your electromuscular system be effective against them."

"Ah!" She began to see the point of his concern, then shook her head. "I still don't figure it. We chanced to land on Carim Carim's ground by the merest accident. We could as easily have come down a couple of million miles away. So how was it that he was prepared for us?"

"I know this sounds ridiculous, but I have the curious feeling it wouldn't have mattered where on the shell we'd landed. Carim Carim was slow to come and find us, but in the meantime he'd have had ample time to receive his instructions and make his preparations."

"The tyrant's instructions?"

"At a guess, yes. I think on Neptune shell we'd be wise to throw away all the experience we've gained with typical shell populations. Neptune's different. They've far fewer people and a higher level of technology than anywhere else in Solaria. Something is upsetting the Solarian norm, and that something could well be the tyrant's influence."

"Carim Carim doesn't look to me to be the victim of tyrannical oppression."

"You're still thinking in the old terms, Sine. Forget them. Keep an open mind. And above all, find out what makes Carim Carim tick."

When the meal was ready, robots came to fetch them. After his recent considerations, Ancor was inclined to regard them more as a guard than an escort. Carim Carim's manner bore no sign of menace, but Ancor was interested to note that each member of the *Shellback*'s crew had a robot which stood directly behind him "to assist at table" in addition to those mechanisms which actually did the serving. Despite the apparent friendliness of the scene, it was not lost on him that this was the first occasion when he had left his whole party so exposed to potential danger.

At the meal Carim Carim, still in his red hat, was expansive and genial.

"I shall call you by your first names, and you shall call me simply Carim. By your faces I can see you're plagued with curiosity, which I will try to alleviate. Maq, suppose we start with you."

"We've been to all the inner shells of Solaria," said Ancor. "But from what little we've seen of the Neptune shell so far, this appears to have by far the lowest population density. Is there a reason for that?"

"Of course!" said Carim agreeably. "We like life and we like the feeling of plenty of space. Unlike other communities of which we've heard, we don't double our numbers every thirty years. In fact, the shell's population has been substantially stable for centuries at around five times ten to the fifteenth power. We've earned our living space, Maq."

Ancor took a moment to compute the figures in his mind. Then: "But that's around ten thousand square miles per person. With such gross overcrowding on some of the other shells, is that justified?"

"There's no moral issue involved. Just because ten people have to sleep in the same room in some shanty slum somewhere doesn't mean that everyone ought to sleep ten to a room. It's all relative, you see."

"But Zeus redistributes population excesses to try and achieve a certain norm. For some reason that system appears to be breaking down where the lands of the Neptune shell are concerned. Carim, what does happen to all the emigrants fetched out by the spokeways?"

"I hope that's a rhetorical question. I don't know what hap-

100

pens to them, because those that go on outwards are never able to return to tell us about it. One assumes that there are other outer shells in Solaria stretching to infinity."

"Then I'll re-phrase the question. Why do the majority of those emigrants who reach here apparently not remain?"

"Ah! The nub of the problem. You suspect some infamous exercise by which we send the emigrants away again. Well you're wrong. All are equally welcome to stay or to continue their journeys outwards, which ever they prefer. We merely explain to them the system and lifestyle by which we live, and leave the choice to them. Nearly all of them go."

"This is ridiculous!" said Sine. "Anyone offered your lifestyle would be crazy to refuse it."

Carim's eyes were resting on her interestedly. "I merely explain what happens. I don't attempt to interpret it. It might be possible we could make the same offer to you, my dear."

"Then I think I know which way the answer would go." She glanced speculatively at Ancor, then returned her attention to Carim. "Just try me!"

"Accepting what you say for the moment," said Ancor scowling in Sine's direction, "we are naturally intrigued as to how you came to know so much about us, Carim."

Carim grinned delightedly. "It wasn't difficult. All we needed was access to the Solarian Identifile."

"Which Zeus won't normally permit."

"The farther away from Zeus, the less absolute its power. And the larger the shell, the more widely spaced are its local executive stations. On Neptune shell anyone with the right equipment can gain access to the Identifile. Because by the time Zeus learns of it, it is too late for it to intercept."

"That's roughly what I'd already figured. So now tell me about the tyrant."

"Ah, the cosmic bogey! The great Solarian myth. There isn't one, Maq. You're chasing moonbeams. Look where you will, you'll never find him. If that's what brought you out to the Neptune shell, you've wasted your time."

"I don't believe you," said Ancor levelly. "Something very strange is happening on Neptune shell, and its repercussions are affecting all the rest of Solaria. Most particularly it is affecting the Uranus shell, which is so overcrowded that its systems are virtually on the verge of breakdown. If the tyrant doesn't exist, then something else does. And I intend to stop it, whatever it is."

"Then I must re-name you Don Quixote Ancor. And Tez I think would make an excellent Sancho Panza. But this silly topic

101

has become boring. Come, Sine, let me show you some of my treasures. Whilst Maq goes hunting windmills, I suspect that you have more sense. Forgetting idealism, let's go and explore some of those things which really make life worth living.''

"He's trying to split us up," said Tez, as Sine and Carim left the room. "Sine wouldn't stay here, would she?"

"I couldn't stop her if she chose to do so. But we aren't seeing the right picture yet. All this is just a gloss, a surface veneer, something trying to turn us lightly aside. But I'm sure that underneath there is something completely diabolical. I don't know what it is, but I'm sure we're not going to like it. Come on you two, let's get back to the *Shellback* and check on those monitors we left running. Something about this crazy set-up has to start making sense fairly soon.''

Meanwhile, Sine Anura was having the time of her life. Rich though the treasures of the household were, they were poor in comparison with those which Carim kept in his private rooms. Here were jewels and necklaces, bangles and ornaments of such excellence that Sine had never before imagined that such a collection could exist. Furthermore, she found Carim uncommonly generous. Whenever she found a piece which was exactly appropriate against the green shiningness of her skin, he insisted on making a gift of it to her. She, too, had gifts to bestow, and with careful art and the faintest hint of sex-attractant pheromones, she wove around him a snare of anticipation which increased his generosity and made his eyes shine curiously bright.

Finally she offered submission to his advances, and coaxed him into an imaginative love-play which left him gasping with delight. Soon his natural level of reserve and control had fled, and he became a creature of passion which she could mould with the same level of skill and artistry as had been used by the hands which had fashioned the fabulous jewellery which now erotically adorned her naked body. Carim was obviously no novice at love-making, but Sine's easy expertise and encouragement was adding a new dimension to the experience, and his enthusiasm knew no bounds.

Then just as he was about to engage her fully, a swift change swept over him. He withdrew suddenly, almost snarling, as though stricken with a mysterious fit. Yet there was no illness there: his eyes were cool and reasonable, and his momentary anger ceased. It was almost as though his whole personality had been suddenly exchanged for another, both sane and balanced but having completely different viewpoints on the question of total abandonment to passion.

Sine looked at him appealingly for a moment or two, found

littlc in him which was the same as the Carim she had led so skilfully only seconds earlier, then succumbed to her own feelings and launched herself at him furiously.

"You impotent bastard!" she said. "Why the hell did you go so far before pulling out? You must have known you were useless."

Carim took the abuse with a slightly philosophic smile, as though the whole affair was a question of very little importance to him, and he certainly did not have the look of a man who has just failed in the making of love. Almost spitting with fury, Sine lashed at the smiling face, and completely knocked off the red hat which Carim had insisted on retaining. And then wide-eyed and screaming with horror she fled from the room, with the image of the dozens of electrodes and the banks of tubes and micro-circuits he had wired across his skull burning in her mind as though impressed with a red-hot iron.

Outside in the *Shellback*, Maq and Tez watched the band of local transmissions flare across the face of the pulse analyser, and wondered just what activities such a strong and complex radio signal betokened.

CHAPTER EIGHTEEN

ESB

SINE ANURA ACTUALLY reached the head of the stairs before a blued-steel robot emerged from one of the alcoves and dexterously seized her by the wrist. She turned to fight it with her free hand, but remembered first to hit the emergency alarm button on the transceiver at her waist. She had scarcely sent the electric equivalent of a scream winging on its way when the robot reached behind her and trapped the other wrist. Its grasp was precise and firm, and the horrifying thought flashed through her mind that it probably had strength enough to completely sever her hands from her arms by merely tightening its grip. She tried to bend her fingers round to touch the metal hands, in case Ancor had been wrong about the ability of her electromuscular system to affect it, but its grasp was too high to enable her to make contact.

Carim, red hat again enclosing the bizarre apparatus on his head, came along the corridor and watched her struggling and there was a thoughtful frown on his face.

"A pity you did that, Sine. As much as I was enjoying it, they didn't dare let you take control."

"What the hell are you talking about?"

"You really don't know, do you? For a while you had a power over me which transcended any external stimulus which is permitted."

"Permitted by whom?"

Carim shrugged. "Maq speaks of the tyrant. He's completely wrong and his ideals are too simplistic, but let's retain the word as a label for something yet to be explained. The tyrant wouldn't permit it. He alone has control over the greater passions of life. He brings the tears and the laughter, the meditation and the apprehension. And the joy . . . Nobody can exceed his influence."

"Apparently I nearly did," said Sine reasonably. "What sort of wired-up freak are you, Carim?"

"You won't understand this, but I am *Homo superior,* a representative of what the whole human race is destined to become."

"Well to me you're still a goddam freak."

Carim refused to be baited. "What you think is irrelevant. You speak from ignorance, and therefore can't judge rationally. When you become one of us you will see it differently."

"Me? Become wired-up like you?"

"It has already been decided. The best way we can deal with your danger is to answer all your questions totally. There is no more effective way we can do this than to make you like ourselves."

"But God . . . you've got wires running into your brain! You're controlled. You're no more than a copulating robot. Are all the people on Neptune shell like this?"

"All of them. And for the good reason that once you've tried it you know there is no better way to be."

"Once you've tried it, you're subject to control. You can simply be instructed to believe there's no better way."

"This argument is useless, Sine. We hear it all the time from the emigrants to whom we offer it as a prerequisite to remaining on the shell."

"I don't wonder they refuse to stay."

"Any advanced society needs to impose restrictions and disciplines upon its subjects if it is to survive. The society you come from does the same. But yours is but an arbitrary point in a chain of succession which leads upwards from uncouth savagery through tribal states and federated nations to us here on the pinnacle. It is irrational to point at some link in the chain and say: "We shall stop here, because that is right and all the rest are wrong.' "

"I would certainly choose a point short of having wires running through my skull."

Carim was losing patience. "Then it's lucky that the burden of choice is to be taken from you. It shall be done regardless. Come!" He signalled to the robot, who began to force the protesting Sine along the corridor.

"Where are you taking me?" she asked, and there was great fear in her voice.

"First we have to persuade your companions to join us. They've gone back to the ship unless I miss my guess. Soon the gallant Don Quixote Ancor will be back on his charger to rescue a maiden in distress. I think if I can secure him I shall have little trouble from the rest."

The robot forced the unwilling Sine down the stairs and towards the hall through which they had entered. She was slightly surprised not to find Ancor already there, because he had had ample time to reach the position since she had activated the emergency alarm. Remembering, however, that he had already estimated the robots as something to treat with caution, she suspected he was playing a more devious game. Carim stayed inside and watched thoughtfully through the doorway whilst the robot forced Sine out into the courtyard in the centre of which sat the *Shellback*.

"Mac Ancor." Carim was using some sort of voice amplifier. "As you can see, I already have Sine. I hold her merely whilst I seek your co-operation. I want all of you to come out of the ship unarmed and with your hands held high where I can see them. If you do so, then I promise you will not be harmed. Refuse, and this girl will be torn apart before your eyes. Carim Carim does not make idle threats."

The seconds passed and nothing happened. The robot's grip on Sine's wrists began to tighten convulsively, causing her to wince occasionally with the pain of it. She could sense that Carim's words were not empty. There was no doubt that the mechanism could tear her apart if so instructed, nor was it possible to see how Maq could possibly secure her release. To effectively destroy the robot who stood behind her would have meant using a calibre of weaponry she could not herself have survived. Other robots were moving into the courtyard ready to restrain Maq, Cherry, Tez and Carli as they emerged, and it was undoubtedly the worst situation into which the expeditionary party had ever wandered.

Finally the door opened and Mac appeared with his hands held high as instructed, and the scowl on his lionlike face was dangerous and uncompromising. Then Cherry came out, clad as usual in white toga and sandals, and his apprehension was such that his chattering teeth caused his goatee beard to quiver alarmingly. Tez looked pale but otherwise unbowed and Carli was in tears. Sine knew that once she had triggered the emergency alarm her subsequent conversation with Carim would have been transmitted to the ship, and the *Shellback*'s crew would already have some idea of what it was to which they were surrendering. Only in Ancor's expression could she read any sign that all was possibly not lost.

Carim Carim shouted: "Sensible!" as the crew assembled in front of the *Shellback*, and came out through the doorway to direct the robots in their task of securing the group. Then an amazing thing happened. A second Maq Ancor appeared from round the edge of the little ship, and ran swiftly towards Carim Carim with his weapon raised. Simultaneously the *Shellback*'s weapons pod blasted the robots who were moving in for the securement, completely irrespective of the holo-images of the humans who appeared to be standing in the line of the bombardment. With the swift strides of a beast of prey, Ancor was at Carim's side.

"Make it let her go, or I'll kill you," he said.

Carim, who had not yet come to terms with the idea of being able to see two Maq Ancors or how there could be anybody left in the ship to gun down his robots with high-explosive fire, could do nothing but stare unbelievingly at the weapon pointed at his head. The robot holding Sine, however, must have had an inbuilt over-ride instruction which caused it immediately to abandon the girl and charge against the life-threat to its master. It never arrived. One of the *Shellback*'s heavy-duty lasers fused its kneecaps solid and it toppled to the ground, threshing violently and unable to make any sensible progress in pursuit of its imperative command.

A cry from a second Tez, still in the weapons pod of the *Shellback,* warned them that robotic reinforcements were being drawn in from the surrounding fields. These ran with an amazing grace and speed, six of them striding together and heading towards where Carim Carim was being menaced by Ancor's gun. Tez dropped half of them swiftly with a burst of s.h.e. cannonfire, but the others were uncomfortably close before he finally immobilised them with the heavy laser. Then robots came pouring in from all sides, and Tez on the cannon and Ancor with his handgun were fully occupied in trying to repel the blued-steel swarm. Ancor shouted to Sine to get herself and Carim Carim into the building out of the line of fire, and Carim went with alacrity, seeing the look in Sine's eyes and the way she held her fingers ready to shock his exposed flesh.

Soon Ancor had to flee into the building too, to allow Tez to mop up the droves of new arrivals using heavier calibre shots than were available from Maq's handgun. For a moment he could see no sign of the two who had gone in ahead of him, then a chance noise caused him to look into one of the side rooms. Sine was on the floor, and Carim Carim, with one of the gun-like stun devices he had had with him on the truck, was standing over her. He wheeled round in the instant that Ancor came into view and made to fire the device at him, but stood no chance. A lifetime's training as a professional assassin had made personal survival a reflex action to Maq Ancor. Without even the luxury of having to think about it, Ancor fired—and Carim Carim, their first and so far only contact with the Neptune shell population, was dead.

Sine came out of her coma after about seven minutes, staggered dizzily for a moment or two, then recovered fully. Her first action was to seize the body of the dead master of the house and remove its hat to show Ancor the bizarre apparatus beneath. He studied it carefully for a long time, whilst she kept apprehensively watching the door in case robots came into the building.

"What do you make of it, Maq?" she asked.

"There's what looks to be a multi-channel communications link here, but the major part of the apparatus seems to be based on ESB."

"What's that?"

"Electronic stimulation of the brain. Those electrodes would be inserted very carefully into certain locations in the brain—into the pain-centre, the pleasure-centre, the sleep-centre, and so on. Almost the whole range of human emotions and functions can be stimulated or controlled using relatively small current pulses applied directly to the brain."

"That's frightful, Maq!"

"It *can* be beneficial. With some people who are ill, intractable pain can be blocked virtually completely by ESB without affecting the normal level of tactile sensation. Conversely, it is said that stimulation of the pleasure centres in the brain can generate feelings even better than the joys of sexual orgasm."

"Is that why Carim got himself wired up—to save on aspirin and women?"

"I guess not. But the point is what was he wired up to? Who pulls the switches at the other end of the communications link? The effects of ESB are insidious. The effects of electronic stimulation of the brain appear to the person who receives it to be utterly natural and self-generated. With a set-up of this complexity, Carim Carim could never have known how much thinking and feeling he was doing for himself, and how much was being impressed upon him."

"But where's the point of it all?"

"Sine, it's the ultimate in tyranny. To be able to control a man not only from outside but also from inside his own mind—and make him actually enjoy and welcome it. There's nothing you couldn't achieve given that sort of power over others."

"I find it rather frightening."

"It is. Think what it has achieved here. A whole vast shell is populated merely by a chosen few who work in complete con-

108

cord with the system. And meanwhile, Zeus' emigration program runs awry because no one who arrives here is willing to sacrifice the thing that makes a man unique—human individuality. We've got to find the tyrant, Sine, and stop him.''

CHAPTER NINETEEN

Crazy! Crazy!

BEFORE THEY LEFT they carried out a brief survey of the rest of Carim's establishment. After the death of their master, most of the undamaged robots had returned to the fields. A few attended to recovering the shattered remnants of their own kind and hauling the pieces away. It seemed probable that a threat to Carim's life was the only thing which triggered a reaction against the presence of other humans, and once Carim was dead their cold logic decided that the trigger no longer operated. Finally even Carim's body was unceremoniously dragged away.

The little 'conch houses' proved not to be houses at all, but robotic workshops of very advanced design. It seemed probable that all of the household's requirements were produced here; the food, the furnishings, drapes, even the works of art and the clothing, as well as the mundane items of daily use. Again it made sense of the fact that there appeared to be no roads on this part of the Neptune shell—artifacts were made locally, and therefore no roads were needed for the distribution of goods as in most communal systems. Presumably most of the basic materials were synthesised from produce grown on the farms and adjacent lands, and the actual demand for metal and things not locally available would have been relatively small. Carim Carim claimed to have lived at Seonasere alone, yet these workshops and the buildings they served were able to provide for many many more. Again Ancor received the impression that large numbers of guests could be and were entertained for extended periods of time.

He began to perceive the idea of a floating "court", a whole collection of individuals arriving simultaneously, staying for a period, and then moving on. Thus Carim Carim would have had no need to join a social circle; periodically the social circle would have come and joined him. Some strange skyborne caravan would one day descend and fill the whole establishment with guests, for which the minutest wants of each individual would be catered for by the robotic household. Ancor began to understand that the Identifile information which had been used to supply their own clothes was all part of the standard system. Everything was known about everyone who arrived, and in this respect they had been treated no differently from the rest.

This was a pattern of living which was utterly unlike anything which they had encountered on any of the other shells of Solaria, and the attractions of life as a continuing series of house parties amidst ample and beautiful lands was as compelling as it was dangerous for the *Shellback*'s crew. Those who lived such a dilettante and pleasurable life were not going to surrender it easily, and if the activities of Ancor and his comrades threatened to destroy the system, then resistance against them could come spontaneously from the whole population. The most obvious way to neutralise the danger from the *Shellback*'s crew was to get them to join the system by equipping them with ESB electrodes in their brains. This Carim Carim had already tried to do, and failed. What the next move against them would be, Ancor did not know, but he was reasonably sure that it would be both severe and soon.

Carim Carim had said that there was not one device on the whole shell specifically designed to kill a man. Since all the population was completely controlled through their brains, this was probably true, because no rebellion against the system was possible. But the earlier use of the power transmitter beam against the *Shellback* underscored the fact that devices do not have to be specifically designed to kill in order to be dangerous, and as the little ship finally lifted into the air, Ancor was running monitors on every conceivable physical effect in order to catch the first signs of a new threat.

"Where are we going, Maq?" asked Sine.

"To the nearest spokeways-terminal. We've been following a course roughly parallel to the one which ran through Zapoketa on Saturn shell. At this point it's about ten million miles away, say two weeks travel if we stay down in the exosphere."

"So long to get there?"

"We could do it faster if we went higher. But then we shouldn't be able to scan the ground in sufficient detail to see if this area is typical. My guess is that all of the Neptune shell is rather like this, but it would be nice to be sure."

"And what about the tyrant?"

"I don't think there's any doubt he'll know exactly where we

111

are at any time. But he'll have to come and find us, because statistically we've no chance whatever of finding him.''

The *Shellback*'s ascent was slow, Cherry taking a long, angled flight-path towards the general direction of the spoke-terminal's location which Ancor had given to him. This relatively leisurely rate of rise towards the exosphere gave them the opportunity to calibrate the scanners and recorders so that they could correctly interpret the nature of the terrain over which they were flying even though the details became less distinct with increasing height. Thus as they rose, even Carim Carim's broad lands shrank to become a relatively minor patch on the great shell's girth, and all the features became minute and then invisible. Soon the distant mountains themselves became an insignificant blur and formed merely part of an unfolding backdrop of ever increasing complexity and ever decreasing detail.

Later a chain of great seas became apparent, but these, alternating with blocks of land, suggested that the region of Seonasere was indeed typical of what they could expect to find on the Neptune shell, and nowhere was there the slightest suggestion of an agricultural belt or one of the vast city conurbations so typical of the other shells of Solaria. Ancor, monitoring the radio signals emanating from the surface was able to confirm that the transmissions were relatively widely spaced and more or less evenly distributed. Only from one direction did he think he could identify the transmissions from one of Zeus' local executive centres, but this was very distant, although the pattern of the signals caused Ancor a great deal of thought.

The blow when it came was utterly unexpected, both because Ancor could not have anticipated its form and because his instrumentation told him lies about the event. It was at a period when they were still gaining height and were at midpoint between two local luminaries; and whilst they were themselves illuminated they were scanning a 'night' portion of the shell. The first indication Ancor had of trouble was when the pre-set alarms on the monitoring computer suddenly screamed a warning. The flowing sets of figures on the screen told Anchor that the *Shellback* had gone into a steep dive, and he shouted for Cherry, who had left control of the ascent to the autopilot whilst he took some rest.

Cherry responded fast, winging back to his control cockpit and savagely examining his instruments.

"It doesn't make sense, Maq."

"What doesn't? Hell, get us out of this dive!"

"The radio-altimeter says we're in dive, but the inertial guidance table and the sighting fix on the luminaries says we're still ascending."

"What!"

"Must be an instrument fault."

"It can't be, Cherry. I've got three independent sensors all saying the same thing."

"I don't care. The inertial reference agrees with the visual fix. We're still climbing."

"That isn't possible. For God's sake, Cherry, pull us out!"

"But . . ."

"Take the radio-altimeter readings as gospel. I don't understand it, but I do know we're lost if we impact at our present velocity."

Cherry sighed, and for a while the *Shellback*'s motors strained as he implemented a sudden course correction. The inertial forces of the manoeuvre pinned them all heavily to the decking, and Ancor could hear Carli cursing in the galley as the meal she was preparing got unexpectedly out of control. Cherry was also swearing when the results of his manipulations appeared not to be having quite the right effect. He did something which appeared to reduce the rate of the flowing figures on Ancor's screen, then morosely sat in his cockpit and said to himself over and over again: "Crazy! Crazy!"

Seeing the figures start to stabilise, Ancor was swift to switch to the visual scanner to try and get a second opinion on what seemed to have gone wrong with reality. Sweat beaded his brow when he realised how close they had come to the surface and at what an acute angle they appeared to have approached it. Such a systems failure in the *Shellback* had never before occurred, and such was the multiplicity of reference points available to the instruments that he would have sworn such a breakdown was impossible. Then he noticed something which caused the breath to stop in his throat. The terrain he had been scanning had been in darkness between two long-period luminaries. Now suddenly the ground was light, but illuminated from such an odd angle that only one answer was possible—the *Shellback* had not dived upon the shell, but rather a portion of the surface of the shell had dived up at the little ship . . .

The impossibility of this dissolved after a few moments of frenzied consideration. Like all the major shells, Neptune was braced and stabilised against disastrous collapse by a web of Exis planes, which were gravitationally impermeable and could therefore prevent the gross mass of material reacting with itself and tearing the shell into random globules of matter. Somehow one of these Exis planes had been altered, and a complete surface slice of the shell, lacking now any gravitational attraction to the main structure, had been thrown off into Hades-space by the centrifugal effects of the rotating Solarian universe. Literally millions of square miles of the shell's surface, to some yet undetermined depth, had been sacrificed in a fantastic attempt to destroy the *Shellback*, and such was the staggering damage which this act must have inflicted on the shell that the desperation which motivated it was only too apparent.

Cherry, whose course of action had fortunately been to head the ship straight out into Hades-space, now found himself driving a vessel which was being chased by a not inconsiderable slice of one of the major shells of Solaria. That the ship had the power to eventually escape from such a situation was obvious, but the psychological effect of being pursued by an uncommonly large fragment of the universe was unnerving to say the least, and even when they had managed to leave the phenomenon far behind and turned again towards the undamaged portion of the shell, Cherry could still be heard muttering to himself: "Crazy! Crazy! Crazy!"

Ancor, for his part, was trying to calculate the damage to the shell itself. He lacked an accurate knowledge of the diameter of the circular slice affected by the Exis plane, but it was a conservative estimate that even with the Neptune shell's sparse population, certainly not less than ten thousand people had lost their lives, and the shock and turbulence which must have been imparted to adjacent areas must have brought great havoc to a very wide area indeed. Such a dramatic action could only have been initiated by somebody who could easily usurp Zeus' control of the Exis fields bracing the shell, and whose supreme power enabled him to take such decisions without reference to the lives or wishes of others. This indeed was the work of the tyrant.

CHAPTER TWENTY

Capture

FINALLY THEY SET a course which brought them back towards the damaged portion of the shell's surface. Ancor wanted to examine the area from which the slice had become detached, and Cherry therefore circled low so as to enable them to gain a better view. There was little to be seen. The Exis plane itself was invisible, and the soil and bedrock had been cut clearly as though with a giant knife, and the surface then honed and polished. Ancor was surprised to find an Exis plane set so shallowly, and this was one more pointer to the fact that the larger, outer shells of Solaria were far less stable than the inner shells, and were therefore more precariously braced. This all added to the virtual certainty that physical principles were against the extension of Solaria out to infinity, although it was impossible to tell how many more shells had actually been built around the Neptune-shell.

Cherry turned the ship once more in the direction of the spoke-terminal, this time deliberately setting a high course to give them maximum warning of any similar form of attack, and incidentally to gain an altitude such that they could make the best possible speed towards their destination. In point of fact he cut the projected fourteen days for the journey back to nearer ten, and no further incidents happened on the way. Then at last, from their high altitude, they saw stretched across Hades-space the golden thread which was in reality the great Exis tube of the spoke seen from a great distance.

Maq ordered a slow spiral descent around the spoke whilst he examined the growing detail of the installation beneath, where the spoke ran completely through the shell from Nepturan-space and the inner shells of the Solarian universe. The situation of the terminal itself was completely untypical, it not having become the centre of a great metropolis as had its counterparts on most of the shells. In fact there were not even any roads in the vicinity, which strongly suggested that enforced emigration, with its attendant transport needs, was not something to which the inhabitants of the Neptune shell were themselves subjected. Zeus had indeed lost control of this shell and its population.

There was nothing about the scene to make the travellers particularly suspicious of a lurking trap. The terminal was set in the midst of unremarkable fields, there was no undue broadcasting activity in the region, and nothing at all to suggest that the tyrant and his colleagues were even aware of the *Shellback*'s coming. They landed in a clear space in a field well away from the terminal building which circled the golden shaft, now a mighty structure when seen from close quarters. Ancor and Sine then made the approach on foot, leaving Cherry to control the ship and Tez to man the weapons pod in case of emergency. It was a curious sensation, approaching a terminal which should have been buried in the heart of a multi-mode transport complex in the centre of a megalopolis, yet which stood in a bare field without an approach road to connect it with the mighty lands of the rest of the great shell. Inside this building probably lay the definitive answer as to why the emigrants who arrived from the inner shells opted not to remain but preferred to continue on their long and arduous trip towards the unknown limits of Solaria.

As she walked with him, Sine Anura felt a subtle change coming over Ancor. His normally alert style was increasing to the hair-trigger response pitch of a hunting animal stalking a dangerous prey. Even his footfall was completely noiseless, and she had the insane idea that the slightest stimulus would cause him to spring like a tiger. She had known Ancor in most of his moods, but seldom seen him so possessed of an unashamed killer instinct, and sensed there was still a great deal about the man which even she did not know. This was Ancor the trained assassin, and the care with which he had prepared both himself and his weaponry before leaving the ship made her feel that she was walking with the most dangerous creature ever to stalk a shell.

All terminal buildings were built to the same pattern, provided by Zeus from a common template. The frontage was curved and carried large glass doors which gave way on to a vast internal concourse on which normally stood the long queues of apprehensive emigrants waiting to be marshalled to the spoke-shuttles. Behind the concourse were the gigantic insertion and unloading spirals along which ran the turntables, large as houses, which imparted or withdrew the spin which had to serve the shuttle passengers as artificial gravity during the months-long trips between the shells. To the right lay stores and maintenance sections, all fully automatic and under Zeus' control, and to the left there was provided an area normally allocated for human administration purposes. Centrally in the space lay the fantastic ends of the great hollow Exis spoke itself, in this case a hole in the floor falling fully one thousand million unbroken miles to the next station on the Uranus shell, and from the ceiling rising sheerly up for some unknowable length towards the outer reaches of the Solarian universe.

Entering the terminal, Ancor summed all this in an instant, looking not for the anticipated but for the different and the unexpected. Three shuttles, now laid horizontally, were on the transit loop, but there was no immediate sign of the emigrants they had presumably brought to the Neptune shell, nor, indeed, was there any sign of any human beings at all. There were, however, robots, probably fifty of them, all blued-steel alloy after the fashion of those who had attended Carim Carim. These stood motionless around the walls, and neither by sight or by sound could it be determined if they were aware or completely deactivated.

Ancor summed each robot shrewdly as he passed, looking for he knew not what signs which might indicate they could possibly burst into independent action, but at no time did he approach close enough that if action had been initiated in the metal creatures he could have been taken unawares. His concentration was such that he seemed to have forgotten Sine Anura at his side, and his direction was towards a ladder which led to a high catwalk and a little cabin atop the control structure, in which gleamed a changing pattern of coloured lights. Sine Anura watched him climb and was uncertain whether to follow him. Then she looked at the dark, mute robots standing round the walls and came to a swift decision not to lose touch with Ancor. As soon as he had cleared the ladder she herself began to climb.

By the time she reached the catwalk, Ancor was already at the door of the cabin, and she noted that his weapon was already drawn. She assumed that somebody was in the cabin, but it was impossible to imagine that they could have been aware of Ancor's coming, so silently had he moved throughout the whole affair. She heard the door burst open under the force of Ancor's foot, and Maq's sudden command of: "Out!" to somebody unseen. She arrived just in time for the emergence of one who came out easily even though Ancor had a weapon directed at his back. He

117

was in the process of saying: "Maq Ancor, I presume." On his head was a red hat exactly similar to that formerly worn by the master of Seonasere, and his eyes were completely unafraid.

He stopped when he met Sine Anura, and his expression was one of interested speculation, as though he already knew something about her.

"And the delightful but deadly Sine herself. If you're going to shock me I'd prefer it was deliciously rather than electrically."

"The option is mine, not yours," said Sine, noting Ancor's frown. "But how could you possibly know it?"

"You people are eternally curious. Can't you understand that exchanging information is our way of life? And equipped as we are," he tapped his hat significantly, "information can be exchanged at all levels, intellectual, artistic and emotional. I too could participate in Carim's joy, though I regret he was not allowed to carry it to fruition."

"That's sick!" said Sine. "What are you, a race of electrotelepathic voyeurs?"

The fellow shrugged. "Why limit the pleasures of the senses merely to those who participate in the act?"

"So it wasn't merely Carim I was affecting when he was forced to withdraw?" she demanded. "Was that why he was stopped?"

"A perceptive question, which I don't think I shall answer." He turned easily, apparently oblivious to the deadly aim of Ancor's weapon. "But the lady does all the talking. I take it that the purpose of your visit here is to find out what diabolical rites we practise on the emigrants in order to persuade them to leave our lovely lands to us alone? Well, you shall have your answers. The number of shuttles actually stopping here has been greatly reduced by Zeus these last few years." He glanced back to the moving lights on the cabin wall. "But the signals tell me that one will arrive in about an hour from now. You shall watch the whole process and judge for yourselves."

"That we shall do," said Ancor. "But I shall warn you as I warned Carim Carim—the slightest hint of treachery, and you're a dead man."

"That's another point about us that you've missed," said the fellow easily. "When you're all part of the same complex entity, individual death isn't welcome, but it doesn't hold the same degree of terror as it would for an isolated psyche like your own. When you die, your whole universe dies, but when one of us dies we lose only an infinitesimally small part of the whole. You were most unwise not to accept the offer to join us."

"Thanks for the concern!" said Ancor drily. "But I think I'll keep my psyche isolated just the way it is."

He let the red-hatted fellow go back into the control cabin, and stood with Sine on the high catwalk from where they had a good view over almost the entire installation. Shortly the whole place began to prepare automatically for the arrival of a shuttle from below. A giant turntable moved ponderously towards the end of the withdrawal spiral, and the great slide, which would take the vertical craft once it had stopped spinning and lay it gently horizontal, ran its holding devices out to their fullest extent. Other mechanisms too were starting to operate, and the whole cavity of the building was filled with the rumble of vast machines awoken as if from sleep. The robots also came gradually back to life, and marched in a dark phalanx to the reception point at which the incoming shuttle would finally be halted. Ancor watched them go with a frown, but since none of them attempted to approach the ladder leading to the catwalk, his weapon remained at his side.

Finally came the moment which was fearful if only because they were seeing it for the first time at such close quarters and from such a high vantage point. The shuttle emerged from the lower tube with a great roar, hung precariously on balanced jets in the middle of the cavity for a moment or two whilst a spinning turntable was neatly manoeuvred beneath it, then it deftly killed its leaping drives and sank neatly to rest on the rotating base below it. With its top still spinning, the turntable and its burden began to move outwards around the great railway of the withdrawal spiral, slowly reducing the speed of rotation of the vessel until, by the time it reached the gross mechanism of the slide, the shuttle had completely stopped.

Very gently the slide brought the shuttle to a horizontal position with its hatch at the side and neatly aligned with the disembarkation platform. At this point most of the robots stepped back, as if to adopt an attitude which was not at all threatening, and only one remained like a sole guide at one end of the platform, gesturing as if to welcome those who would step out. It was an organised scene and one calculated to be without any apparent form of menace. Somehow they had to introduce the subject of voluntary submission to surgically-implanted ESB controls as a precondition for being allowed to remain on the Neptune shell, and they had to do this in such a way that virtually none of the emigrants would ever consider it. As the vacuum seals broke open and the hatch began to swing, Ancor leaned forward to try and determine what the initial approach would be.

A second later he said: "Damn!", and his fingers virtually

119

flew to his weapon. But he was too late. By the time he had seen the red hats on the heads of those who had come to the hatch, he and Sine had already fallen victim to the stun devices which they came out firing.

CHAPTER TWENTY-ONE

Interesting Alternative

"MAQ, ARE YOU awake yet?"

Ancor stirred and opened his eyes. He was either in complete darkness or else he was blind, and he had no way to determine which. His arms were secured to a bed by webbed bands at the wrist, whilst a further band crossed his throat. His body felt naked, though covered by a single sheet of cloth, and his head was clamped in a padded block. By the tone of his muscles he could judge that he had been unconscious for a long time, but more than this, what really stamped cold terror into his heart was the sound of Sine's voice. It entered his brain . . . but not through his ears . . .

"Wired up . . . Christ! Sine, are we wired up?"

"I don't know. It's dark, and my head is in a vise. But I can hear you, though not naturally. I've been hearing you for hours talking in your sleep. God, but I'm scared!"

"If it's any consolation, Sine, those we've seen wired up for ESB don't seem to resent it. In fact they appear to regard it as the only way to be. It could make an interesting alternative to death. It's just that . . ."

"Just what, Maq?"

"We're individualists, Sine. And for us the loss of individuality would be even worse than death."

"What can we do?"

"I'm going to try and break out of this thing I'm in. If I have been wired-in and there are still connections, then I'm liable to do myself some damage. But I have to try."

"Don't do anything foolish, Maq. Wired or not, where there's life there's still hope. We need you."

"I *have* to try."

He lay there for a moment or two logically considering his

position. If he had judged the feel of the band around his wrists rightly, then there was little chance that he could break it without a lever. It was a question, then, of how it was secured—by buckle, clip or screw, and whether the fastening could be persuaded to slip a little. He concentrated on his right wrist and despite the awkwardness of the angle he assisted his arm muscles with what leverage he could exert with his fingers against the framework of the bed. For a long while he strained in the darkness, and the force of his exertions was such that he could feel the blood pounding in his temples.

Then finally something gave, only a little but sufficiently that his hand, trained in the assassin's art of escaping from manacles and handcuffs, was finally able to withdraw through the loop. The pressures he had exerted must have weakened something in the mechanism, because his left hand was more easily released, and then he was feeling over his shoulders for the one remaining clasp which secured the band at his neck. He found a clip with a knob on it which he managed to turn, and the coupling came free. Now he was faced with the harder decision—how slowly or swiftly to remove his head from the clamping block, and how to know when any damage he caused himself became irreparable. His fingers told him nothing except that the hair had been shorn from his neck and that his head was probably shorn, but the close enfoldment of the block prevented any further examination until he actually withdrew his head from it.

"This is it, Sine! Win or lose, I have to try."

"I know you have to. You wouldn't be Maq Ancor if you didn't. Best of luck, Maq!" Though her words seemed confident, fear inhabited the edges of her voice.

He bent his knees, gripped the sides of the bed securely, and drew his head out of the block. Apart from a sudden chilling as his scalp came out of its cosy confines, nothing happened. Sitting up, he swiftly examined his head with his fingers. As he had guessed, his head had been shorn—but the scalp was unharmed, and none of the dreadful electrodes had been attached.

"Sine, I'm all right. I think we could both be all right."

His tone was one of sheer relief. There was, however, no answer at all from Sine.

"Sine, did you hear me? I said I'm all right."

Again no answer.

He considered this silently for a moment or two, then was struck by a sudden thought. Dropping back on to the bed, he pushed the top of his head into the slightly yielding block until it fitted into its former position.

"Sine, do you hear me now?"

122

"Sure, I hear you. What's happening?"

"I took my head out of the block and nothing happened. Nothing has been attached."

"Marvellous! So we're still in with a chance. Can you get me out too?"

"I'll try, but I don't know where the hell you are. With my head out of the block I couldn't hear you, nor could you hear me. So I guess we're not in the same place."

"Hurry, Maq. I've a feeling something's going to happen."

Ancor, too, felt the tension rising, and swiftly sat up to check the environment around him. He thought he heard some slight noise, moderately distant, but it was too indistinct to be deciphered. Intending to look for a light of some kind, he swung himself off the bed . . . then reacted in instant panic. Where he had judged the floor should be his feet had encountered nothing, and a sheer trained emergency-reaction caused him to cling to the bed edge whilst his feet sought purchase on the latticework on which the bed was supported.

"Sine, this is unholy! Someone's taken the floor away," he said, although he knew she could not hear him.

The unlikeliness of this situation puzzled him greatly, and summoning all his nerve he began to climb down the trellis column. He estimated that he descended about thirty feet in the darkness before the situation changed. Suddenly one foot, searching for its next secure position on the regular scheme of crossed diagonal metal rungs, encountered the cold shock of water, and he withdrew it sharply whilst he considered the implications. He felt his mental image of the scene to be wrong, but in his mind's eye he had the impression of a room half-filled with water, from which there rose a thirty-foot lattice tower on the top of which was a bed. One thing the incident told him, however, was that he was not blind. Slight traces of darting fluorescence in the water suggested that some small acquatic creatures were in the area into which his foot had dipped. On a suspicion that they had been attracted by the scent of human flesh, Ancor descended no further. After pausing for an agonised re-appraisal of his situation, he began to climb back again towards the bed.

"Sine!" he felt her mentally jump when he made contact with her again through the head-block. "This place is weird. The bed's on a tower, and beneath it there is water with some fish in it. And I still don't know how to get to you."

"I get the feeling we're undergoing some sort of testing, Maq. Perhaps to find out at what point we'll break."

"They won't break us, Sine."

"Maq, I nearly did break. When you went—wherever—on the tower, I got so frightened that I screamed."

"That wasn't you, Sine. That fear was impressed through your head-block."

"I know it wasn't me, but it felt like me. There's no way of distinguishing between real fear and artificial fear. Even the comfort you're bringing me now, how much of it is real and how much of it is amplified. Suddenly I don't know myself anymore."

"I see the headblocks as removable versions of the head-set which Carim Carim wore. This is the way they offer a sample experience to the emigrants. Then they give them the choice— surrender your minds and stay, or keep your own identity and go. It's not difficult to see why so few of them opt to remain. Even now I think they're feeding in the fear again."

"They are, Maq. I can feel it."

"Then let's try and beat it. This system has to be two-way, because I can transmit to you, and you to me. I want to try an experiment in positive feed-back. What's the best love-session we ever had, Sine?"

"After we first saw the sun in the centre of Solaria, I'd say."

"I agree. Let's both think about it. Concentrate on that hour, Sine."

"Nothing would give me more pleasure."

The first thing Ancor experienced was a sudden flare of fear and insecurity, but sensing its synthetic origin he attempted to ignore it, and concentrated all his mind on the memory of one far incident which had happened just after he and Sine had first seen the natural sun which had brought life to the whole of Solaria. Soon the clawing fears were conquered, and, with his own emotions reinforced by those of Sine Anura, the clear remembrance of those long tides of passion strode through his mind like the waves of some mighty ocean. Again the nameless fears clawed back and tried to drive the loving sequence from his mind. Had he been alone with the image, Ancor felt that the apprehension might have won; but when he faltered, Sine's intense passion buoyed him through, and when her emotions seemed in danger of being crushed, he was somehow able to succour her. Thus it was that the two of them were able to swing the whole image together, and soon the impressed fears stopped coming.

Then suddenly there came a change. Some new and injected emotion began to reinforce the pleasurable memories of that hour of earnest trust and consolation, lifting it to a new height of sensory appreciation. Sensing the uplift, Ancor suddenly cut his imagination short, and knew that Sine was doing the same: overriding human sensations were one thing, but artificial stimulus was a game in which neither of them wished to be involved. For them, reality was the only thing which counted.

Despite their voluntary withdrawal from the contest, the pleasurable sensations grew and grew, seizing their bodies like a powerful drug, almost addictive in its sensory fascination. Ancor could hear Sine moaning softly as the deepseated stimulation of the pleasure centres of her brain was brought about by neutral currents impressed through her skull. He found his own mind enshackled by sensations more pleasurable than anything his corporeal senses could provide, but he had an advantage not available to Sine—the power to lift his head voluntarily out of the fateful head-block.

Though he would have hesitated to admit it, the decision was probably the hardest choice he had ever faced. On the one hand he could remain incumbent and delight in the realms of a pleasure greater than even his own prime body could provide: aternatively his assassin's instinct shouted a cry of danger, warning that, as in some patterns of drug addiction, the indulgence of the moment would have later to be paid by subservience and degradation. As the sensations swooped towards a new sort of climax he made his choice. He withdrew his head from the pleasurable block, and sat up to face the cold, harsh realms of reality.

Somebody shouted: "Bravo!", and immediately there was light, and he was staring through a glassy cover to where the fellow he had encountered in the terminal was looking down at him from an adjacent gallery.

"You're a rare fellow, Maq Ancor! There's not many who could or would have broken out of a pleasure-pulse like that. What made you break away?"

"I have an abhorrence of bondage. What are you doing to us?"

"Demonstrating the advantages to be gained from ESB and our collectiveness through close communications. You showed that you, too, shared these needs. When you drew your head out from our inductive cap, you lost touch with Sine. It was your voluntary wish to put your head back in again, in order to find the close comfort of another mind. You climbed down the tower and came back, and then your need was to communicate and to share the experience. Finally you collectively re-lived a moment of an old memory, but instead of just re-telling a story you were able to re-experience the heights of its pleasures even though your bodies were separate. This isn't bondage, Maq Ancor, but rather an extension of the human mind."

"I think 'invasion' of the mind is a better word."

"In your terms all sensory inputs are an invasion of the mind, inasmuch as they cross the interface between the brain and the outside world. The burnt finger makes us jump, music can bring us joy, or drama lead us to tears. A succulent meal can bring us pleasure, or a fragrance stimulate the imagination. ESB is merely another bridge across that necessary boundary between brain and body."

"Not so," said Ancor. "The mind and the body evolved together, a psychosomatic entity, each part serving the other. But ESB can bestow joy where there is nothing to be joyful about, or pain where there is nothing against which to react. It can bring fear in the midst of security, and unholy calm when there is a need to fight. It makes a travesty of human experience."

"We had hoped to convince you to join us voluntarily," said the fellow sadly. "But it would appear that your ways are set. But join us you will, Maq Ancor. Though now we must do it without your consent."

CHAPTER TWENTY-TWO

Breakout

THE LIGHT COMING in through the cover some six feet above his head enabled Ancor now to check the impressions he had formed in the darkness about his place of confinement. He found they were basically true. The "bed" was on a lattice tower, and this could apparently be raised or lowered. Also there was water beneath, covering the entire floor to some undetermined depth. The room or cell was probably a pit with sides about fifteen feet across and fully thirty feet in height, and everything about it spoke of considerable age. Had he been assured that it had been in use for centuries he could easily have believed it.

Noting his interest, the man with the red hat spoke again.

"You seem puzzled by our methods, but historically there are very good reasons for the design of such a cell. Firstly, it was cheap to construct, and we needed a great many to cope with the influx of emigrants who used to arrive here. Secondly, it's escape-proof. Over the years, many have broken their bonds as you have done, but none have ever broken out. Thirdly, although we haven't insulted your intelligence with it, the table on which you lay can be rotated and dropped and angled in combinations which in the darkness can be completely disorientating. Thus nearly separated from the normal physical sensations of reality, a man retreats back into his head, so to speak. And it's there in his head that we meet him. It's there we make the point that sensations and emotions don't have to coincide—that even disorientation can be highly enjoyable and that stasis can be sheer hell. The power of ESB."

"And the water?"

"Most people have a morbid fear of slow drowning. The acid test of ESB is that a man can be filled with laughter at the instant he thinks he is going to drown."

"Where's the point of it all?"

"To demonstrate the disciplines required by a superior society. A savage coming into your way of life would not like to have to wear shoes, pay taxes, or submit to governmental control. He has to surrender some of his native freedom if he wants to gain the advantages your society has to offer. The step to our way of life is no different. You surrender some freedom of the mind in return for the advantages our society has to offer. It's a difference of degree, not of kind."

"Not to me it isn't," said Ancor sourly. "What happens now?"

"The operating rooms are being prepared. This will take a little time, because they are very little used these days. Then you and Sine Anura will be taken and fitted as we ourselves are. After that, there will be no more dissension between us. Excuse me, but I must go and see that all is going well."

He disappeared from view although the light remained. Ancor forced his head back into the block.

"Sine!"

"Listening, Maq. What's happening?"

"They are preparing to operate on us. I have to find a way of breaking out of here. Don't worry if I'm not in contact for a bit."

"Is there a way out?"

"Not at the bottom. I guess it's a pit sunk solidly into the earth. But there's a glass cover above which they must have opened to put me in here. I'm going to try and get through it."

"I'll have to leave it all to you, Maq. I can't even move. Good luck!"

Standing on the bed, Ancor could easily reach the transparent cover with his hands, but the exercise did not encourage him. The material was not glass but probably an organic plastic and it felt very tough and thick. He realised that without tools he was going to find it virtually impossible to break through, and his red-hatted captor must have known this else he would not have left Ancor unobserved.

Maq then began to examine the structure of the bed, looking for something he might be able to tear off and use as a crowbar. He climbed back down the diagonal lattice, examining the linkages which enabled it to be raised and lowered, but it was too well engineered to be taken apart by hand. Finally he looked up underneath the platform of the bed itself and found something which had previously escaped his attention. A neat row of six switches, probably for engineering test purposes, had been arranged beneath the platform at the head of the tower, and their positioning was such that he would never have found them had his captor left him in continued darkness.

Careful inspection showed him that they were labelled, but the symbols he did not understand. Experimentally he depressed one, and it was an instant which nearly cost him his life. The tower went into such a violent spin that, being unprepared, he was thrown clean off it, bounced against one of the walls, then dropped like a stone into the water. Fortunately the tower stopped its violent rotation after about half a minute, and the water had been deep enough to cushion his fall. He swam strongly for the base of the tower and hauled himself out in desperation, but not before whatever creatures which lived in the water had had the chance to draw blood from his lower limbs. Safe again but chastened by the experience, Ancor began doggedly to climb back up the tower towards the fateful switches.

Again he studied the symbols on the labels, but was unable to guess what function each controlled. Reaching through the lattice as he had to do in order to reach the controls, he was uncomfortably aware of what might happen if he depressed a switch which sent the tower into swift collapse—he would be trapped and lose at least two limbs and possibly his head. Then he thought of the operation which was being prepared for him and Sine Anura, and a peculiar kind of fatalism came over him. Whatever the cost, he had to try.

He had reasoned that he had been introduced into the cell with the transparent cover drawn back and the bed raised to the level of the gallery above. What he needed now was the switch which would restore the bed to that same height. The panel told him nothing of the logic in its designer's mind when he had decided to place the switches in a particular sequence. Was the second one for rotation in a reverse direction, to angle the bed, or what? There was no way to find an answer except by trial, and his own body on the metal lattice would amply pay for any mistake. He had pressed the first switch of the six and survived by being lucky. He now pressed the last.

This time the movement was slower but very positive: the tower was extending. Soon the bed was pressed up against the transparent cover, and he could hear some distant motor change its note as it encountered the resistance of the material in its path. Estimating what might happen if the great sheet above him fractured and fell in shards, he pressed himself through the lattice so that the bed on the top gave him at least partial cover. Then to his dismay the rise of the platform was halted, possibly by the stalling of the drive which powered it. In anguish he touched the switch again and the motor responded, but only for a short period. He tried the operation repeatedly, and thought he could feel the tower extend slightly each time, but it looked as though his great idea was not going to work.

The vast splintering crash as the transparent cover failed was his final and unexpected reward, and the plunging fragments fully justified his forethought in seeking cover against them. The material was thicker than he had supposed, and many of the falling pieces were large enough to have ripped his body open had they struck him. Relieved of the opposing pressure, the tower continued to extend, and stopped when it was level with the gallery. Even before it had fully come to rest Ancor had climbed back on to the bed and leaped on to the gallery rail at the nearest point available. He was challenged immediately. The breaking of the cover brought a blued-steel robot running. Unclothed and without weapons, Ancor had no choice but to engage it in unarmed combat exactly as he would have tackled a man. Although it was heavy, he managed to turn both its weight and momentum against it, and it followed the fragments of the cover straight to the bottom of the pit.

Ancor searched swiftly then, fully expecting further robots to appear, but none came. The gallery was in a six-sided room, five sides of which were lined with equipment, and the sixth gave directly in to a corridor which obviously served a double row of such "cells" and was so long that in one direction he could not see its ending. In the other direction about six cells away the corridor became a broad ramp which sloped upwards out of sight, and Ancor guessed that this led directly into the spoke-terminal and would be the route by which the emigrants were brought down to be given their encounter with the effects of ESB. It was probable that Sine was not very far away, but rather than search for her as he was, Ancor's most urgent need was for a weapon with which he could hold his own against any men or robots he encountered. He knew he had been lucky with the robot which had tumbled into the pit, but that was not the sort of luck which was liable to hold.

He moved swiftly towards the ramp, wondering where his own possessions had been placed when they had been taken from him. He found nothing to suggest a likely place to look, and continued on up the ramp hoping to establish his bearings. Soon he could see ahead of him a high roof, and he knew that his guess that the way led into the spoke-terminal was correct, but whether he could cross it and safely reach the ship where he had a plentiful reserve of arms was a matter about which he had the gravest reservations.

He was nearly at the head of the ramp when the completely

unexpected happened. There was a great, thunderous crashing sound, and he distinctly felt the walls of the building shake. Simultaneously there was a burst of cannon fire, so close and loud that Ancor could have sworn that the gun was actually inside the terminal itself, although he knew this to be impossible. A man with a red hat went rushing past the upper end of the ramp, stopped in sudden shock, then crumpled doll-like to the ground. By the time Ancor reached him a simple glance was sufficient to establish that the fellow had been killed by a high-velocity pellet, and the marvellous truth began to dawn upon Ancor. Somehow Cherry had contrived to drive the *Shellback* completely through the glass frontage of the terminal, and had actually landed the ship inside, from which position Tez in the weapons pod was now placed to take control of the entire establishment.

CHAPTER TWENTY-THREE

Kyns Ala

GETTING TO THE *Shellback* safely had been a major problem, because Ancor minus clothes and minus the flowing mane of red hair was not immediately recognisable to the ship's crew. He waited on the ramp until the lessened firing suggested that Tez was reasonably satisfied that nothing dangerous remained on the concourse or behind it, then he rose and with hands raised and choosing the most open route he could find, he walked deliberately towards the ship. Tez put a couple of warning shots over his shoulder before it dawned on him that the strange fellow walking towards them was none other than Ancor himself.

Then things moved swiftly. Carli opened the hatch and helped him in, and Ancor seized a work-suit and a fresh set of weapons. Then he called Tez from the weapons pod and armed him likewise.

"Sine's still trapped downstairs, so we have to find her and get her out. Tez, you come with me. Cherry, you take over the guns here. Shoot any robots and anyone who wears a red hat, but otherwise conserve your ammunition. I don't think you'll have any trouble."

Cherry looked apprehensively at the firing mechanisms in the pod and seemed about to say something, then he saw the look in Ancor's eyes and changed his mind. He knew perfectly well how to operate the cannons, it was just the noise he did not like. Carli then pushed herself to the fore. She was seldom asked to play an active role in the exploits, but she was quite proficient in the use of a handgun for self-defence. Now she looked at Maq questioningly, and he nodded his agreement. If Sine was to be rescued, he might well need all the backup he could get.

Before they got back to the ramp another red-hat appeared, coming out of the storage section and holding a stun device.

Through the support piles of the insertion spiral he was a difficult target for Ancor, but he must have been in clear view of Cherry, for the cannon spoke once and the man literally dissolved in a hail of fragments. The little holo-illusionist was apparently taking no chances, and was using projectiles of a far higher calibre than the situation demanded, but Ancor was interested to note that his aim was completely true.

Then they were on the ramp, descending down to the long corridor which served the chains of cells as far as the eye could see. It was a marvellous place for an ambush because they would be exposed to the aperture of a cell on either side before they had the opportunity to discover whether or not the cells were occupied. However, they passed ten sets of cells without incident, and leaving Tez to guard the way in front, Ancor called Carli back to guard the foot of the ramp.

"To find Sine I shall have to go into each of the cells and look down into the pit. And when I do find her, it may take a while to figure out how to release her. Cover me while I check these ten cells, and if she's not there we'll have to work our way down the corridor."

Carli nodded and looked apprehensively up the slope of the ramp. Her handgun was loaded with s.h.e. pellets which was the only calibre of ammunition usable in a sidearm which stood any chance of stopping a robot. The trouble was that even in Ancor's skilled hands, it did not always stop them, and they could run remarkably fast. Ancor searched swiftly, scanning through the pits, trying to find out which one was occupied by Sine. He was struck by the fact that when he had been in a pit the darkness had been absolute, whereas the lighting in the corridor would have thrown at least some illumination through the cover. Working from one side of the corridor to the other, he covered the first eleven cells, including the one from which he had escaped, and then found one on which the cover was opaque. This appeared to explain the mystery of the light. Somehow the cover could be made transparent or light-proof, probably at the touch of a switch.

"I think I've found her." He called Tez and Carli closer to guard the door, and set about examining the controls. The relative ease with which he had made his own tower-bed break the cover sounded a note of caution. If he initiated the same sequence in Sine's tower without finding out how first to draw the cover back, he stood a fair chance of killing her by compressing her against the cover. Rather than risk this, he crossed the corridor to where the pit was empty, and began to try the controls at random. Soon he hit the sequence—cover transparent or opaque, cover across or withdrawn, and tower lowered or extended. He then went back to the cell with the opaque cover and rendered the sheet transparent.

Two eyes looked up at him with agonised apprehension, but they were not Sine's eyes. A male of perhaps twenty-five lay strapped on the bed with his head in an inductive block, and it was clear that his impressed sensations were certainly not happy ones. Ancor swore and made the cover withdraw. Soon he had the bed level with the gallery, and was able to release the man's bonds and instruct him on how to draw his head out of the block. Shortly the man, sheet knotted round his waist, was standing slightly belligerently by Ancor's side.

"You won't make me do it!" he said positively, feeling his shaven head. "I'd rather die first."

"You'll be pleased to know that I'm not trying to make you do anything," said Ancor. "We're on the other side. You an emigrant?"

"Yes, Kyns Ala, from Uranus shell."

"Many of you here?"

"There were a hundred and fifty in our shuttle."

"And they were all brought down here?"

"I assume so. They knocked me out with something. When I woke I was in that—that place." He nodded towards the pit. "They told me what they wanted, but I couldn't accept it. Not wires in your head . . ."

"I felt the same," said Ancor. "Look, Kyns, I've no time to explain now, but my friends and I are staging a revolution against the head-tappers. If you'd care to join us, come along. We've a chance to get all the others out, but it could be dangerous."

"I don't care. I'd sooner die than do what they say. I'm with you."

"Good! I'll show you how to operate the switches, and we'll work our way down the corridor and release everyone we can. But we'll have to be quick, because I suspect the red-hats will soon be sending in robot reinforcements."

As he spoke there was the loud sound of gunfire in the corridor. A quick appraisal told him that a robot had descended the ramp, and had been destroyed by Carli with her handgun. There was still a trace of disbelief on her face at the effectiveness of her fire. Ancor made only the briefest introduction of their new colleague, and then they were away rapidly, exploring further cells along the corridor. Kyns Ala was a quick learner, and soon found out how to identify which cells were occupied and how to release the victims safely. He was also a good organiser, and had some of those emigrants released earlier form a backup team to explain the situation to those just released, freeing Ancor and himself from the necessity to stop for repeated explanations. He also ensured that the growing group of liberated men and women stayed as far as possible inside the entrances to the cells in order that a continuous watch could be kept along the length of the corridor and firepower applied whenever a robot appeared.

If there were any more red-hats in the area they had hidden themselves well, and only about a dozen robots were encountered. Most of these fell to Tez and Carli, though Maq himself took two which had run uncomfortably close. A group of emigrants tried to tackle yet another with their bare hands, and three men were torn apart before Carli managed to get in a lucky shot which immobilised it. It must have been Kyns Alá who found Sine Anura, for soon she was back at Maq's side, and helping with the release of even more emigrants, who now seemed to be occupying virtually every cell in the row. Ancor had lost count of the number of people which they freed, but it was certainly more than one shuttle could have carried, and his final estimate was that close on three hundred people had been drawn out of the pits. He had come down to the corridor looking for Sine Anura, and unexpectedly finished up with an angry and determined army. Certainly the tyrant was not going to be pleased.

Finally there were no further people to be found, and they judged all the rest of the cells to be empty. Maq called then for an orderly movement back along the corridor and into the terminal, he and Sine leading the way, and Tez and Carli covering the rear. There were no further incidents, however, but Cherry's amazement was great when he saw the unexpected multitude emerge from the ramp on to the concourse.

Ancor then drew Kyns Ala and his swiftly-appointed lieutenants aside and explained to them as much as he could of the situation on the Neptune shell. Coming, as they all did, from the vastly overcrowded shell of Uranus, where there were something approaching a hundred thousand people to the square mile, there was astonishment that here on Neptune shell a single person could have ten thousand square miles to himself. They all immediately decided they would stay on Neptune shell and fight for a fair proportion of the available space and resources.

Ancor wished them well, but there was a frown which never left the corners of his eyes: he knew that here he was watching the birth of a new nation, but new nations are invariably born out of bloodshed, and baptised by want and fire. Many of these before him would never live to see the brave new future they had

135

in mind; and if they succeeded and multiplied they could fill even the vast girth of the Neptune shell to capacity in around seventy generations.

Taking the existing shell population into account, and assuming that emigration from other shells might soon be restarted, the capacity of the Neptune shell to absorb any more of the overflowing tide of humanity in Solaria would be spent in a thousand years, and possibly in as little as five hundred. Supposing the battle to wrest control of the Neptune shell from the hands of the tyrant was eventually won, it would still have little impact on the horrific overpopulation problems facing mankind in the rest of the Solarian universe.

And the battle itself had hardly begun.

CHAPTER TWENTY-FOUR

Information

IN THE STORES section of the terminal they found ample supplies of the type of food normally provided for prolonged spoke-shuttle trips. The emigrants were heartily tired of such fare, but at least it ensured that no one would actually starve for a while. Knowing the tyrant's propensity for committing large-scale acts of destruction when attempting to get rid of minor embarrassments, it was Ancor's opinion that Kyns Ala should divide his force into three separate parts, leave one-third at the terminal to assist any new emigrant arrivals, and send the other two parties as far away as possible in different directions, so that any mammoth blow against one group would be unable to damage them all. Kyns Ala listened carefully, but did not agree. Although he had been told of it, he had still not psychologically accepted the vast scale of the slice of the Neptune shell which had been detached and liberated into space in an attempt to destroy the *Shellback*. In any case, he was having his first taste of power, and was in no mood to receive suggestions. Having estimated the capabilities of some of the men who had arrived with Kyns, Ancor knew it would not be long before his position as leader was challenged, but he forbade to comment. It was nothing to do with him.

Kyns Ala first asked for and then demanded to be provided with weaponry from the *Shellback*. Ancor studied his reserves and decided he could make none available, whereupon Kyns let drop a hint about thinking of acquiring the whole ship. Ancor located and demonstrated four of the stun devices which had been left by the red-hats, and Kyns Ala was thoughtful. The group which attempted to approach the *Shellback* after local nightfall ran into a barrage of searchlights from the ship, and had to move quickly to avoid the back-flux of its jets as it rose from its position on the floor of the terminal and was gone. Only one point arising out of the previous three days of discussion did Ancor feel bound to keep, and that was a promise to attempt to reach one of the adjacent spoke-terminals and repeat a similar operation there. The only item of the *Shellback*'s equipment which he did leave behind was one of the small radio transmitter-receivers, so that they could keep in contact at least until the little ship was out of range. As they rose into the air, Ancor tried the call frequency, but judged the set to be unattended. The emergent nation, he thought, was going to have a lot to learn. He would have liked to have stayed to see how they fared, but it appeared that politics were already outstripping survival sense.

His main interest at that point was the nature of the reactive strike which the tyrant might decide to employ. It was not lost on Ancor that the entire terminal and the threat it now represented to the tyrant's ultra-totalitarian regime could be completely eliminated by the application of a relatively small nuclear weapon, and this probably without detriment or danger to many of the red-hatted inhabitants. It was to avoid the disastrous consequences of a move such as this that Ancor had advocated that the emigrant force be divided. Now he directed Cherry to bring the *Shellback* to a hover-mode a mere ten miles above the terminal, and for a further three days they watched for an event which fortunately did not happen.

According to calculation, the next spoke-terminal was some fifteen million miles distant, a projected trip of three weeks' duration if they stayed in the low exosphere. They could have done the journey far more quickly if they had gone right out into Hades-space, but Ancor wished to keep the ground at least under partial surveillance. In point of fact, it was a journey they were never to make at all. Having decided that it was unlikely that any missiles were now likely to be projected against the terminal, and that their own anti-weapon resources were not required, Ancor directed Cherry to prepare a course for the flight, and, checking that his scanners and monitors were working, he returned to the computer to review some of the accumulated data.

NEPTUNE SHELL: LARGEST KNOWN SHELL IN THE SOLARIAN UNIVERSE, ALTHOUGH LARGER SHELLS ARE PRESUMED TO EXIST.
MEAN DISTANCE FROM SUN 2793 MILLION MILES
DIAMETER 5586 MILLION MILES
CIRCUMFERENCE 1.75 TIMES 10 TO THE 10TH POWER MILES
NUMBER OF CAGEWORLDS: 480 LESS 1 DESTROYED

Memory of the cageworld which had been sacrificed when the *Shellback* had first arrived was suddenly coupled with the recollection of the surface slice which had hurled itself into space in a similarly fruitless attempt to destroy the expedition. Having met Carim Carim and several other red-hats, it did not now appear likely that they were the type of men to participate in such momentous and desperate decisions. So now he was looking for the tyrant, and the tyrant had to be completely different from his underlings. How different? Primarily, he could usurp Zeus' functions totally provided he could achieve his object before Zeus could find out and respond. Look at that point again.

MEAN DISTANCE OF NEPTUNE SHELL FROM SUN 2793 MILLION MILES

MEAN DISTANCE OF ZEUS FROM SUN 67 MILLION MILES

MINIMUM SIGNAL PATH: NEPTUNE-ZEUS: 2726 MILLION MILES

SIGNAL TRANSIT DELAY TIME (MINIMUM) 4.07 HOURS APPROXIMATELY

On the face of it, the tyrant would have four hours in which to initiate an action before Zeus got to know about it, and a further four hours must elapse before Zeus could countermand the order. There was, however, a flaw in that reasoning, and that flaw concerned the massive size of the shell itself. To bounce a radio wave completely round the shell would take twenty-six hours, and if the tyrant was on the opposite side of the shell from the event he ordered, thirteen hours must elapse before he could start to get things done. Yet Zeus could learn of the decision and countermand it in only eight hours!

Ancor sat up sharply and looked at the figures with renewed interest. The mathematics were not in favour of the tyrant. In fact, depending on where he was located, he could effectively oppose Zeus only over a fraction of the shell's surface. But what if there was more than one tyrant? A brief consideration showed that there would need to be about eight to give them reasonable control of the shell, and even then the advantage would be minimal in the peripheral regions around their respective locations. Ancor then called in Cherry, who had similar problems with interference fringes between holographic projectors when creating large terrain holograms. Cherry was no mathematician, but there was nothing he did not know about the properties of light, and his goatee beard waggled excitedly as he plunged into the largest calculation of his life.

There were no exact answers to the equation: it all depended on the degrees of effectiveness you required to achieve. Cherry had his own "gullibility factor" which he used for such purposes, which depended on the psychological impact of the holo-scene to distract attention from slight technical imperfections in the image itself. Because Maq had asked him to handle the problem as though he was creating (Heaven forbid!) a global terrain hologram of shell-sized proportions, Cherry threw in his "gullibility factor" for good measure, knowing sadly that in so doing he could have created areas of visual garbage probably several millions of miles across had it ever been built. His only solace was that it would never be put to the actual test.

Finally he handed his tentative calculations to Ancor, who seemed more than a little surprised.

"Eighteen hundred? I hadn't thought so many."

"Depends on the definition you want to achieve, and your average viewing distance. I wouldn't care to do it with less, and even then I'd have to be very careful where I sat the customers."

"Thanks, Cherry! At least you've given me something new to think about." Ancor examined Cherry's calculations carefully, and something about the spatial separation of the holo-projectors caught his eye. He returned to the computer, fed Cherry's figures in, then began to re-run records of patterns of the broadcast transmissions they had been collecting since their arrival on the shell, looking for near coincidences. He found one almost immediately, and as he sat looking at it his eyes grew wide with a sudden speculation. The figure of one thousand seven hundred and ninety-one was the projected shell total for the number of transmitters of a very distinctive kind, and the more he thought about it the more certain he became that he was looking into the face of the tyrant of Hades.

"Cherry!"

"Yes, Maq?" Slightly miffed by Maq's apparent lack of enthusiasm with his figures, Cherry had retired to his control cockpit to check on his instruments.

"I think you could have cracked the problem for us. I've changed my mind about the flight destination. I'm feeding new co-ordinates through to you on the data line."

"Receiving them, Maq. What's out there?"

"I'm not quite sure, so I want to have a look. Keep us in the low exposure so we've an opportunity to monitor anything happening on the ground. Tez, keep the weapons panel open from now until I say otherwise."

"What's happening?" asked Sine Anura, suddenly becoming aware of the increased activity.

"We predicted that in order for the tyrant to be fully effective in usurping Zeus, he would have to be operating from a minimum number of points around the shell. Cherry made it eighteen hundred. The interesting fact is that there just happens to be around that number of a particular type of radio transmitter operating. So we're going to take a look at one of them. With one pinpointed, we can find all the rest with tolerable accuracy."

"Will that lead us to the tyrant?"

"If what I suspect is right, it will. But the tyrant can't fail to be aware that we're on to him. And from that point great troubles could arise."

"What sort of troubles, Maq?"

"Think what we've learnt about the tyrant, Sine. He's completely ruthless, and apparently prepared to sacrifice everything and everyone in order to hit at us. And his powers, even if they aren't absolute, are getting very close to it. If the tyrant is who and what I think he is, then fighting him would be akin to taking on God himself."

"Co-ordinates set in, Maq," said Cherry. "Estimated time of arrival over the target area approximately sixteen hours from now."

"Right! That gives us just about time for a thorough ship check. Carli, run a stores update. Sine, come and stand by these monitors and let me know if anything shifts towards the red. Tez, check your armoury, and keep a selection of weapons primed and ready for immediate use."

"And what will you be doing whilst we're doing all the work?" asked Sine Anura.

"I'll be on the computer and the radio. I still haven't cracked the codes they use for the fantastic amounts of data they transmit around the Neptune shell, but the transmitter towards which we're heading has a code pattern which looks nearly familiar. I've just remembered that we've an ally who should be rather good at solving problem codes."

"An ally?" Sine was perplexed.

"Sure. Zeus itself. All the indications are that the reason we're here is to do its dirty work—we're a sort of technological cat's-paw. We can do what Zeus can't do for itself, simply because we're on the spot. As I see it, the least it can do is to back us with information."

"How can you get in touch with it?"

"That shouldn't be too difficult. It must be monitoring virtually every damn radio signal on the shell. If we go out on open transmission on several bands, I think there is every chance it will hear us."

"But will it reply?"

"That we shan't know for at least eight hours, because it will take that long for our signal to reach it, and for us to receive its reply.''

Eight and a half hours later Ancor was proved right. A local transmitter on the Neptune shell surface contacted the *Shellback* on its own call frequency and sent a coded request for a data transfer link. The ship's computer responded automatically, and for the next two hours a veritable flood of digitised information flooded into the memory store. Ancor sampled some of the incoming information occasionally but realised with a shock that the sheer volume of it would occupy a whole human lifetime in order to comprehend it. When the transmission was finished, however, his own computer signalled its readiness to decode any Neptune shell broadcast that Ancor cared to designate, and from that moment Maq began to feel he had a slight chance of winning.

CHAPTER TWENTY-FIVE

Storm

"TROUBLE!" SAID CHERRY sharply, after a time.

Sine Anura concurred. "Jet-stream, Maq. High velocity movement of the upper atmosphere."

"At this height?" Ancor moved to where she was frowning over the monitors.

"Hey, that's quite a storm! Some of that stuff must be doing thousands of miles an hour. Fortunately the atmosphere here is so rarefied that there's very little mass actually involved. Is it affecting us, Cherry?"

"Not much at the moment. Slight frictional heating on one side is about all. But you should see what's waiting for us down below."

"Oh?"

"What we're reading here is only the high-altitude margin of a giant rotating storm. And currently that has its centre somewhere round those co-ordinates you gave me."

"Mm. Sounds like the tyrant does know we're after him." Ancor bent over his instruments. "Ah, I see what you mean. Looks a hell of a mess down there. Any idea what's causing it?"

"I once saw a blow-up something like that when I was on Mars shell. Apparently one of the luminaries altered its output and this drastically upset the weather pattern for the whole sector."

"That could figure, because the tyrant would have control of the spacekeepers tending the luminaries—at least until Zeus could take corrective action. But luminaries keep travelling, so he'll find it difficult to maintain the storm in that one location."

"Sure. But when the influence of that luminary has passed, all he needs to do is tackle the next one in succession. If he can't hold the storm in one place, at least he can sweep the area with a chain of storms. As far as we're concerned, the effect could be much the same.''

"How bad is it down there, Cherry?"

"Too bad for us to venture into, Maq. Once the *Shellback* gets down into the atmosphere it becomes subject to the same forces as any other atmospheric craft. If what the radar backscan tells me is true, we'd be tossed around like a piece of tissue paper.''

"We have to get down there somehow. Once you're over the target area, hold your position and maintain altitude. We'll monitor the storm and check the periods of the luminaries for this latitude. There has to come a period when the storm can't hold.''

"Any way you want it, Maq.'' Cherry sounded dubious but took over manual control and began to alter the instructions which had been fed into the automatics. Ancor took a sighting on the local luminary which was in clear view overhead, and coaxed his instruments into providing him with a definitive spectroanalysis. Initially he could find little wrong with the results, then a discrepancy came to light.

"The damn thing has been doped,'' he said. ''Somewhere out there is a spacekeeper feeding in some elements completely foreign to the requirements of that type of proto-star. In point of fact it has driven the output up by only a few percent, but that's enough to play havoc with the chemosphere and the weather below. And there's not much Zeus can do about it now, because once such elements get into a proto-star plasma they can't be removed selectively. So that storm is going to travel a fair way round the shell before the effects are dissipated. At a guess the next luminary along the line is also being doctored.''

"But it's significant that the storm only started as we approached this particular region,'' said Sine.

"It is indeed. There's no doubt it was done deliberately to keep us out. It's the same pattern we've seen before. The damage to things on the surface of the shell will be massive, and out of all proportion to the problem it's designed to solve. A fantastic, paranoid over-reaction, completely without regard for the consequences. Whoever or whatever the tyrant is, he's completely insane. It's almost as though he's prepared to destroy whatever he possesses rather than give up the idea of absolute possession.''

Sine Anura was looking at Maq searchingly. ''Perhaps he doesn't regard the shell in the same way as we do—as living space for people. You had an idea in mind when you brought us to this spot, Maq. Who do you think the tyrant is?''

"Not so much a tyrant as tyranny. There can't be just one

tyrant, because one couldn't communicate fast enough to beat Zeus over most of the shell. So how do they manage to usurp Zeus' command of the mechanisms which serve and maintain the shell? That could only be done by gaining control of Zeus' local executive centres which attend to the day to day routines of shell maintenance."

"So?"

"The interesting fact is that the optimum number of tyrants appears to correlate very well with the projected number of local executive centres. I suspect Zeus' own super-intelligent remote executives are in revolt against their master."

Sine Anura considered this thoughtfully for a moment.

"But couldn't Zeus handle that itself—just switch them off or something?"

"Possibly, but then the whole system would break down. Zeus can't maintain the shell by remote control because of the four-hour delay between order and execution. That's the reason the executive centres exist—to interpret Zeus' long term policy and take fast action locally. If Zeus switched the executives off, the shell would die, and so would all the people on it. And as widespread as they are, we're still talking about five thousand million million people."

"And what about these people—all wired-in red-hats, if we're to believe what we're told. As you asked before, who pulls the switches at the other end of the ESB communications link?"

"I think the answer is pretty plain. It's the tyranny that pulls the switches. As I see it, on Neptune shell both people and machines are interlinked. That's what the tyrant is—one vast bio-electric complex. Don't ask me how it got started, but once it did get started it was unstoppable. If a group of citizens decide that they, their children, and any new arrivals will all be wired for ESB, then once the pattern becomes established it can't be broken. They must always win because they have instant communication with their neighbours and can even summon robots to their assistance over the radio link."

"I hadn't realised they could do that."

"Remember at Seonasere, how the robots came in out of the fields. And how they lost interest when Carim Carim died. We only escaped from that through Cherry's holo-trick and the fact that we were heavily armed. Those are two advantages that most people on the Neptune shell do not possess."

"So accepting that this bio-electronic monster has been established, what's the point of it all?"

"For the machines, never having to be concerned with the main problem which besets Zeus—what to do about an ever-

145

increasing population. Anyone who submits to ESB control can't contribute to a population explosion.''

"How do you figure that?"

"Carim Carim said the population of the Neptune shell had been stable for centuries. As we know, that's unlikely to happen naturally. The reason for it is that the tyrant can read the level of sexual interest in a man's mind, and can switch it off, as you yourself have observed. Control sexual desire, Sine, and you can fine-tune a population for absolutely zero growth.''

"It's an original approach to birth control," admitted Sine. "And what do the people get out of belonging to the complex— apart from a sense of frustration?''

"They live literally like lords, and all their material wants are well provided. From their viewpoint, it's a very good arrangement. On the whole I imagine they lead more pleasantly balanced lives than anyone in the whole universe.''

"You sound as though you're making out a case for them, Maq.''

"There is a good case for living in total harmony with your environment. But I doubt there's a case for your environment having the power to make you live in total harmony with it.''

"The storm centre is moving on, Maq," reported Cherry. "But conditions are still pretty desperate down there. Perhaps in an hour it'll be quiet enough for us to attempt a landing. But there's another storm following, so we'd not have more than two clear hours on the ground before we have to fight our way up again.''

"Two hours mayn't be sufficient. I don't know much about Zeus' local executive centres, but since on most shells they handle the emigration enforcement program I can't imagine they're easy places to get into.''

"What's the point of trying to get in?" asked Sine. "Why not just drop a diffract-meson warhead on it from up here?''

"Two very good reasons. Firstly, this is only one amongst hundreds. Secondly, we daren't destroy it completely for the same reason that Zeus can't switch it off. For all its faults, it is still serving a useful function in keeping part of the shell maintained.''

"What could you do if you could get in there?''

"I'm interested in the part that contains the human communications and ESB control system. This could never have been any part of Zeus' original specification, so it must have been added, or at least adapted from something else.''

"Why do you want that piece in particular?''

"If we could learn how to break or short-circuit that link, five

146

thousand million million citizens on Neptune shell could be returned to near normality even if they did still have wires in their heads. Cherry, you've got to find a way of getting us down there as soon as possible. I don't even know what it is we're looking for, but we should be able to home in on its radio signals.''

He went back into the computer bay to sort out a few sample transmissions which they could use as a positional reference. In doing so, he looked up at the screen and saw that one of the transmissions was actually being decoded by the computer, utilising the information which Zeus had placed in the memory store. The first banks of figures were probably machine addresses and three-dimensional space co-ordinates. Secondly, probably derived from an electronic thesaurus which made a rough human translation of the ultra-precise machine language, there came the interesting phrase: DESTROY OR BE DESTROYED.

Ancor could gain no idea for what or whom this message was intended, and he could have been over-fanciful in imagining that it applied to the *Shellback* and its crew. Somehow, he did not think he was wrong. The presence of the *Shellback* in this location, and its confinement to a high altitude by the chain of successive storms which ran below suggested that they had correctly identified the nature of the tyrant and had been branded as a unique threat. It was a situation in which virtually anything could happen.

"Starting the descent now, Maq," said Cherry. "But if things prove too rough I may have to back off. Storm-wind at ground level is still reading in excess of five hundred miles an hour, and I daren't approach the ground whilst it is in excess of two hundred.''

"Do the best you can, Cherry. Every extra second you can buy me on the ground will be worthwhile. If we leave it until the wind drops lower we'll have even less time before the next storm hits.''

"Reading you, Maq. I'll have a go.''

"Sine, you'll come with me. Full work-suits complete with masks. It won't be easy to breathe in that wind pressure. Tez, you stay with the guns. I doubt if there'll be anything to shoot at, but we daren't take chances. And we'll maintain continuous radio contact all the way.''

Ancor felt the nudge as Cherry trimmed the motors and started the descent, but the factor which really caught his attention was the startled flare of the figures and messages on the screen. The executive centre below obviously knew every phase of their movements, and suddenly it was scared. Amidst the jumble of figures and numbers, the electronic thesaurus snatched occasional words and phrases which had a direct equivalent in the human language. There was no syntactical sequence in the display, but the message was one of abject fear and panic. With grim humour it occurred to Ancor that any red-hat within the range of these transmissions would be having a pretty unhappy time right now.

CHAPTER TWENTY-SIX

The Egg

WHATEVER THE FIGURES on the gauges read, Ancor had to admit that Cherry's natural caution was justified. Despite the power of the *Shellback*'s jets, once they encountered the full force of the storm the little ship was twisted and thrown about as if it were a piece of paper. Bravely the holo-illusionist at the controls tried to head her into the storm, but the upthrust of vagrant winds forcing against the randomness of an unknown terrain repeatedly struck the ship at an awkward angle, and, momentarily reinforcing the action of the downthrust jets, threatened to flip the vessel right over, with completely disastrous results.

More than once Ancor was on the point of abandoning the landing attempt, but the fortitude with which Cherry tackled the control problems and the sign that the wind was indeed lessening, caused him to opt for a continuation. From the messages of acute alarm he was reading on the screen he decided that he had indeed located the tyrant's Achilles' heel, and he wished to press home this advantage if it was humanly possible. Indeed, it was the human element which was the complication. The *Shellback* was designed to take many times the amount of punishment it was receiving, but for its relatively fragile crew the ordeal was of a different class entirely. The violent heaving and bucking of the ship, with its unpredictable lunges and changes of direction, was a direct threat both to life and limb. Even where the crew were confined by safety straps and webbing, the motion was such as to produce the most uncomfortable form of nausea as the ship constantly rose and fell and spun as though tossed on the waves of some unimaginably frightful sea.

Virtually ignoring his instruments, Cherry was attempting to play the game by instinct, dropping the ship lower to sample the fury of the turbulent effects, then frequently returning to some higher altitude in order to retain control. Thus they made their slow descent, stepwise, gambling on the signs that the worst of the storm was abating and that there would come a couple of hours of relative calm before the fury of a new storm descended.

Despite the fantastic variety of environments through which the little ship had travelled on its journeyings, it was this descent through an atmospheric storm which most brought home to the travellers the stupendous powers of natural forces and the relative fragility of man. Even the hull, normally quiet with the vast silences of space or the upper atmosphere, began to shriek with the passage of the wind around the projections on its ugly non-aerodynamic form, and though the ship was completely airtight it was difficult not to imagine that the sharp winds had penetrated and were moaning and twisting through the complex installations of the ship itself.

Even Ancor had to admit that Cherry's mode of approach was probably the most effective that could have been devised. The holo-illusionist's natural timidity led him to back-off immediately he experienced the sudden panic of feeling control of the ship slipping from him, and in this respect he was more finely tuned than the best instrumental system which could have been applied to the task, acting often with a gifted anticipation born of natural fear which uncannily detected a pressure ridge which the sensors had not had time to perceive. It was obvious that the storm was dropping, but this was purely relative. No structure not securely bolted to the ground could have resisted the slam of a five-hundred mile per hour headwind, especially a headwind which died within seconds to leave an area of rarefaction into which the *Shellback*, although theoretically buoyed by reactive thrust, tended to drop like a stone. Only the massive inertia of the vessel helped to slow the violent patterns of acceleration and decline and keep the internal forces—just—within the limits of human tolerance.

Slowly the storm-force continued to reduce, and as it did so Cherry dropped the *Shellback* ever closer to the ground. Whilst the upper atmosphere had been crystal clear, the lower approaches were different. Here, great stormclouds being drawn into the vortex were being shredded into streamers of sullen lead, white above and murderously black below. And as the clouds were racked and torn asunder, so freak weather conditions were produced as a response. High-level electrical storms with discharges completely within the thunder-cells, lit the sky like explosions in some ghastly aerial war, and the strength of the lightning pulses was such that the *Shellback* would have been vapourised entirely had one chanced to strike her directly. So too

150

with massive atmospheric ice; whole clouds were coalesced and driven down way below freezing point by some sudden, violent pressure change, to produce massive shards of flying ice which rattled off the *Shellback*'s hull like bullets and did much damage to the small antennae and some of the more exposed sensors.

Then came a relative lull, the wind force dropping to around two hundred miles an hour and becoming comparatively steady both in force and direction, and thankfully Cherry nosed the craft against the wind and began the final part of the descent. They were fortunate indeed that the course they had been forced to follow in combating the storm had not caused them to drift too far away from their intended target, and now with only relatively minor corrections Cherry was able to home on the battery of the radio transmissions which were emanating from somewhere yet unseen on the ground.

If Ancor had hoped for good visibility at ground level, he was to be sadly disappointed. The tortured stormcloud above, as if to avenge itself on the cause of its anguish, sullenly refused to permit anything but a dull parody of twilight to reach the ground. Meanwhile the violent rainfall, saturating the wind-torn surface, had contrived to produce a sea of mud from which an ochre spray of nearly complete opacity was being torn in sheets by the prevailing furies. Cherry levelled the ship nearly fifty feet above the surface, being unwilling to approach closer until he was prepared to make a firm landing in case some unexpected squall should rob him of control and dash them violently to the ground.

"We're down, Maq—nearly. And the transmissions are lined-up dead ahead. You tell me when to land."

"Thanks, Cherry, will do. You know, there were times when I never thought we'd make it." Ancor was in the observation bay trying to scan ahead for any features which might give him a clue to the nature of their destination. The visibility was terrible. He cut in the large searchlights, but these only accentuated the flying yellow spray and actually made the situation worse. Additionally, even at fifty feet above the ground, the driving mud was accumulating on various parts of the ship, and only the occasional rain-squall cleared the viewports sufficiently to give him a few moments of water-wavered view before the determined yellow turbidity marched back. Only the monitors confirming the radio fix dead ahead seemed lucid and self-sure.

Then suddenly a structure loomed ahead and he sounded to Cherry a note of caution, but the latter had already seen it for himself. The thing that they were approaching was a gigantic metal "egg" fully two hundred feet in length and one hundred feet across at its widest point, which stood out of the slushy sea of the terrain on six curved elephantine legs. As he regarded it, Ancor remembered that he had seen such things on other shells but had never before stopped to consider their particular function in Zeus' control hierarchy. In many places on the shells there were entirely automatic installations devoted to aspects of shell maintenance, and the nature and relationship between these was little understood by the human populations. They were generally regarded as being virtually impregnable and potentially highly-dangerous devices with which to interfere. Because of the unpopularity of the enforced emigration programs on certain shells at particular points in history, attempted attacks on Zeus' installations had once been frequent: in consequence Zeus had "hardened" its defences against man's interference or spite. Ancor now realised that he was faced with the consequences of this policy. He needed access, but since the installation would be entirely automatic and self-repairing, there did not actually need to be any way for a human to get in.

Perhaps the tyrant was also an untouchable. A sense of frustration welled strongly in Ancor, but it was not in his nature to give up without a fight.

"Where do you want me to attempt a landing, Maq?" Cherry's guarded question was phrased with a respect for the glutinous and apparently unsound nature of the terrain.

"Close as possible to the legs at this end, Cherry. Between them, if you can."

Cherry studied the prospect. "Hell of a risk in this wind. If we get thrown against one of those it could crack the hull."

"I'll leave it to your discretion. Do the best you can."

Cherry brought the craft in low, well clear of the mighty egg, and tested the terrain. To his immense relief he touched solid bedrock only a few inches under the surface ooze. He presumed that the original soil covering must have been stripped clean by the wind, and that all that now remained were stubborn tailings and water. Emboldened, he inched the *Shellback* forward, grounding occasionally when he felt the pressure of the wind begin to drive him off his chosen course. Finally he had the craft within inches of Maq's required position, and thankfully he cut the motors and felt the grav-locks bite into a solid base beneath.

"All set, Maq. But whatever you do, don't take too long. If the wind starts rising again, we are going to have right trouble getting out of here."

Whether Ancor heard him was uncertain, because he and Sine, in full work-suits and carrying coils of rope and other implements, were already in the lock and preparing to leave. They used the space-lock rather than the simple hatch in order to stop the storm-fury breaking into the interior of the ship when the outer hatch was opened, because despite this being the lowest-key weather they had encountered on their approach it was still a storm by any normal standards well beyond the range of human experience.

His job finished temporarily, Cherry moved to the observation bay, from where he could vaguely see Ancor emerging from the lock. A mammoth thunderstorm was raging overhead, and in the dim light, its multiple pulses of bright electric fire lent to Ancor's movements a kind of irregular stroboscopic effect in which he appeared to move jerkily from one position to the next and was barely visible between. Then coming out of the lee of the ship the full force of the wind caught Ancor squarely, tore him bodily from the treacherous ground, and hurled him staggering and floundering out of sight behind one of the giant legs of the egg. Holding his breath Cherry had to wait a long time for the next lightning pulse before he was able to see the taut-stretched line which still connected Ancor to the grapple-bars by the hatch. As was his nature, the assassin was never one to take unnecessary chances, and in this instance his caution had probably saved his life.

Soon Sine Anura, a brilliant auxiliary lamp slung around her neck together with further coils of rope, could be seen fighting her way down the line, frequently slipping but always managing to regain her precarious equilibrium and never for a moment losing her handhold. Finally she too went out of sight behind the leg.

The thunder blared yet more violently, the intermittent gusts of wind drove like hammer blows, and the ship rocked occasionally despite its solid moorings. Cherry returned to his cockpit and began to monitor the progress of the next storm, the outriders of which he estimated must reach the area in two hours at the most. Whatever Maq had to do would have to be done quickly if the ship was ever to be safely lifted away. Cherry now realised why the ship shuddered every time it was hit by a squall—the grav-locks were holding but the bed-rock into which the ship was secured was friable and already beginning to break away.

And on his scopes was the clear image of a new storm.

CHAPTER TWENTY-SEVEN

The Key

BENEATH THE BELLY of the great egg, Ancor had already begun testing, but what the instruments told him he had already guessed for himself, that he was looking at a shell of hardened space-alloy at least a foot thick. Using the *Shellback*'s heavy duty lasers it would be possible to cut through it, but the internal damage would be enormous, and he dared not risk incapacitating the executive centre completely because of its function in controlling the life-supporting systems for this part of the shell.

In order to position himself to take the measurements he had cleverly managed to use the force of the wind itself to aid him in wrapping a strap completely around the nearest of the giant legs, and it was to this that the line to the ship and his own work-suit safety lines were now attached. Even though thus secured, the irregular gusts penetrating beneath the egg's belly and around the crouching *Shellback* not infrequently threw him off his feet, and he blessed the foresight which had caused him to don the tough and padded work-suit which had already saved him several times from a disabling injury. Equally important was the mask. Although intended for work in vacuum and poisonous environments, it was here utterly necessary in order to protect human lungs from the pressure of the wind which would otherwise have rendered breathing difficult or impossible.

Whilst he worked and stumbled he could see Sine working her way along the ship-line, the bright auxiliary lamp bucking and rearing as the gusts tried to tear it from the lanyard round her shoulder. She was carrying most of the heavier items he had thought they might need, and his heart went out to her because he knew that if she lost her footing she must fall more awkwardly and on to more bulky packages. Fortunately she had her suit harness looped to the now taut ship-line and was able to recover her position even though occasionally laid nearly prone by the glancing spite of the gale. Finally she staggered to his side and clipped her safety harness to the strap. Both of them were now completely covered by the flying mud, and fully fifty percent of their time was spent wiping their visors in order to be able to see.

"Anything yet, Maq?" At least radio communications were not being affected by the sedimentary spray.

He tapped the egg significantly. "Space-alloy. We could cut it open if we had to, but only at the risk of destroying it entirely. But even if it is self-repairing, it would still need extra stores occasionally, so there ought to be some sort of hatch. The problem will be to find it."

She looked up at the vast bulk of the egg. Like themselves it was coated with dripping mud, from which the petulant squalls ripped an occasional sheet of blinding spray.

"That could be a long job, especially if it's located high up. We could never search it all in this weather."

"The best we can do at the moment is look around. If necessary we'll have to come back after the next storm."

"Are you sure this is the only way?" She looked forlornly at the vast bulk above them, dripping ooze from all sides. "Even if there is a hatch, it's unlikely to be easy to open. And if it's not designed for human attention, nothing is going to be prettily labelled anyway, so we won't know what we're seeing."

A sudden blast of pressure sent her staggering and finally falling on to her back, whilst Ancor held his position only by hanging grimly on to the line. Even he had to admit now that the situation seemed hopeless. With some risk they could make their way around the other five legs and examine a small portion of the bottom of the egg, but that was about their limit. Whilst the storms persisted there was no way in which it would ever be humanly possible to examine the sides or the top of the giant ovoid sphere. Nor was it even certain that there was anything to find. The tyrant had played a master card.

Or had he? The squeals of cybernetic fright which the executive complex had transmitted at the *Shellback*'s approach had to have some supporting reason. If the egg was truly impregnable, then what did the device have to fear? This time it was Ancor who went down under a sudden burst of flailing wind, and as he lay on his back magnificent chain lightning of incredible intensity lit the scene continuously for fully half a minute. And in that time he saw something which his tentative exploration with

155

the auxiliary lamp had failed to reveal—the inside of the leg to which they were strapped exhibited a toothed vertical rail.

This curious fact merited some attention. It was unlikely that the whole egg was constructed so that it could raise or lower itself on its own legs, and the only other answer seemed to be that the rack was designed to allow some other mechanism to ascend at that particular point. Focusing the auxiliary lamp and directing it at the second leg of the pair revealed that this was similarly toothed, and it was probable that the missing mechanism actually ascended between the pair.

Taking the lamp from Sine, he turned the beam vertically and began to examine the bottom of the egg directly between the legs. Muddy spray repeatedly lashed across his visor and spoilt his view, and in attempting to reach an area just beyond the limits to which the safety lines on the harness would allow him to go, he ill-advisedly unclipped the lines and released out. It was a badly-timed move. The gale suddenly reached an unaccountable burst of malevolent fury, driving storm-rain so furiously that it hit him like a solid wall and sent him staggering backwards, twenty feet, thirty feet, until he was brought to a halt with a bone-wrenching jar against one of the centre legs; and the auxiliary lamp, flying on its lanyard, struck the metal with such force that its strong case literally exploded, and the lamp was dead. But the incident had had its encouraging side also. As the storm water had hit the base of the egg it had momentarily flushed the wall clear of mud and he had clearly seen the outline of a small hatch cover in the bottom.

Sine had given a little cry as she watched Ancor hurled away, and had immediately attached a further safetyline to the belt to enable her to go to his rescue. It was Cherry, however, who now monopolised the radio link.

"Maq, we've got problems here. The bed-rock is tearing away from under the grav-lock. We're at an awkward angle and that last blast nearly stood us on end."

Ancor's voice sounded strained as he answered, and a second or two had to elapse before he regained his breath.

"Would it help if you shifted to a different position?"

"Yes, but there's no way we can do that without breaking your safety line."

"Then you'd better break it. I think we're on to something here."

"No, Maq. This wind is getting worse again. The second storm is still a way off, but we seem to be seeing a reaction between the two. I want both of you back aboard immediately."

"Taking charge, are you, Cherry?"

"In your absence, I'm the ship's captain, Maq. I know what I'm saying. I can see the instruments, and you can't."

"You're perfectly correct, Cherry. We're on our way."

After a great struggle to correct her direction on the end of the second line, Sine Anura reached Ancor, and together they fastened a belt around the second leg. Whilst they were doing so it became quite apparent that Cherry was telling them no less than the truth. The wind was increasing drastically. They coupled their safety harness lines together then, so that each could aid the other, and began four-handedly to haul themselves back towards the ship. Frequently they lost more ground than they gained as the punishing squalls, almost solid with driven rain, repeatedly dislodged one or other of them and sent them sprawling. Gradually, however, they forced their way inch by painful inch, at least until the first leg had been gained, and if Cherry needed any confirmation of the earnestness of their efforts he need only have listened to their laboured breaths over the radio.

As they neared the first leg, Ancor looked up, and the scene, lit by one amazing pulse of lightning, made him point breathlessly to Sine. On the hatch was a small handle which, by jumping, he could just reach. Risking being caught by the driving gusts, he leaped up and put all his weight on to the handle. After a second or so some reluctant spring gave way and the hatch came open on a hinge to reveal a cavity disappointingly far too small to admit the passage of a man. Inside it, scarcely now protected from the vagaries of the weather, lay something which gleamed bright and golden in the lightning's prancing flare. Ancor looked at it, recognised the splines of a multi-way electrical connection, then had to drop back to the ground. Then he and Sine were literally fighting for their lives as the wind rose to unprecedented heights and dealt them such punishment that Maq began to fear that the suits could no longer give them adequate protection, and against the force of which even his own trained muscles were powerless to move.

In the end it was Tez and Carli who saved the day. Donning another suit, Tez came out of the hatch with a winchrope round his waist. As he advanced down the ship-line Carli paid out a limited amount of rope from the winch until his welcome hands encountered those of Sine Anura. Then slowly, against the bitter crescendo of an ever-increasing gale, she towed the floundering figures back to the threshold of the hatch. Thankfully they thrust themselves inside, but were not a moment too soon. As Cherry had said, the wind-force was lifting the ship bodily, and a very little further increase in the speed of the gale would have sufficed

157

to lift the little vessel from the rear and leave it nose-down against the egg, from which position recovery would have been remarkably difficult.

As soon as he was assured that the hatch was safely closed, Cherry gunned the ship back violently, trying to gain sufficient clearance from the structure of the egg to prevent the rising wind throwing them bodily against it. The irregular, thrusting pressures were against him once the precarious hold of the grav-locks had been released, and it was only the brute strength of the *Shellback*'s motors which enabled him to make any headway at all. But it was a violent, unstable motion which, none of the crew having had time to seek the safety straps, threw them all cruelly about until they gained the sense to lay prone on the deck. Then, seizing what he considered to be an opportune moment, Cherry applied a downthrust, and the little ship staggered upwards into the turbulent air. Ancor, who had found time to reach the observation bay where the monitors were still operating, winced as a gust which Cherry could not have predicted caught the ship and literally threw it towards the unyielding mass of the egg.

The little holo-illusionist at the controls, however, had been wiser than Maq had allowed, and the flux from the downthrusters literally cushioned them from actual contact with the dreadful metal structure. Then they slipped safely over its top and were away into unencumbered airspace. Immediately, the task was easier. The *Shellback*, now riding with the winds instead of fighting them, rose swiftly towards the upper atmosphere. Only twice was she caught by the great random currents, and Cherry handled the situation with patient tenacity, knowing that their ultimate safety lay in the vast stillnesses of exospheric space.

As the crisis lessened, Ancor returned to his computer and began to try and decipher the messages still emanating from the stormswept executive centre below. The centre was strangely quiet, issuing only routine mechanical orders, and the hysteria which had earlier possessed its circuits was absent. It was at this point that he began to suspect the intervention of the hand of Zeus itself, and he turned back to attempt an analysis of the recorded data which Zeus had transmitted into the computer's memory store.

As before, his mind recoiled from its utter complexity, but this time he began to perceive that it had sections and a plan. As a starting point he chose the plan and watched it through without grasping more than a fraction of its meaning. It ended, however, with something which struck an immediate note of familiarity. A dot matrix came up on the screen, and in symbolic representation behind it was the clear outline of an opened hatch. So the flashing points on the matrix could well be a guide to essential terminals on the multi-way connector beneath the egg. Zeus was giving them a key, if only they could discover how to use it.

CHAPTER TWENTY-EIGHT

Fireball

"WHAT IS IT?" asked Sine Anura, eyeing the matrix on the screen.

"Something I hadn't thought of. We've seen these executive centres before. They're a standard item common to all the shells, and are probably made pretty far to sunward. They must be installed when the shell is first constructed, and later programed by Zeus for their particular maintenance tasks. I think Zeus must have had some sort of machine which climbed up those legs and mated with that coupling we saw in order to insert the program. Then presumably it went on to another for the same purpose."

Sine scowled thoughtfully. "That seems a terribly awkward way of doing it. Why not program by radio transmission?"

"I've been wondering about that. Perhaps Zeus has already faced similar revolts on the part of its executive centres. Radio transmissions can be jammed or falsified or mimicked, but a physical connection would be positive. And only two things could reach that connector—the machine which was designed to do it—or something as versatile as a man."

"Us?"

"It would explain what we're doing here, and it would be a damn good reason for what all that garbage is doing in our computer memory banks. I think we've been given a corrective program which Zeus wants us to feed into that egg."

"It might have been more explicit on the point."

"It probably credits us with having far more intelligence than we have. It must be very difficult for a multi-mega IQ device to really understand the relatively limited way in which we think. But I think the message here is plain enough. According to the matrix only seven of those pins are active. Somehow we have to make a connection to them and feed in what Zeus has dumped into our memory store."

"Go down there again?" Sine looked at the instruments monitoring the second great storm as it marched below. "Even Cherry's supposed lull between storms was pretty hairy."

"Nonetheless, we have to try. There's no chance that we have a connector to mate with that one, so I'll have to wire those pins individually. That will take around fifteen minutes under those conditions."

"And how long to run in the actual program?"

"From the volume of what's sitting in our store, I'd reckon another two hours at least."

"There's no way we could sit there that long, Maq. Not if the weather's anything like last time."

"We may not need to. If we take out one of our small receivers and wire that into the connector, we can leave it down there and feed the program in by radio from a safe height. Go help Cherry monitor the storms, Sine, and see if you can figure a safe slot in which we can make another landing. I'll try and work out what we need to take with us."

Ten minutes later she returned. "We've figured a slot in the storms, Maq. I admit it isn't ideal, but it's probably the only chance we'll get."

"What makes you say that?"

"The long-distance radar is fairly jumping with images. Huge craft coming in out of space. The scanners can't resolve the further ones, but the nearest are definitely spacekeepers and the like. And every damn one of them is targeted on this area."

"Ah, so the tyrant's fetching up his big guns! Any of them close enough to interfere with our descent?"

"No, but I'd guess there'll be plenty waiting for us when we try to pull out again."

"Then we'll face that problem when we come to it. Ask Tez to come and give me a hand with this equipment, and get Cherry to take us down into that weather slot."

"Even if we did succeed," said Sine, "I still don't see how reprograming one executive centre is going to affect the rest."

"Neither do I, Sine. But Zeus obviously regards this as a better approach than switching them off. And who am I to argue with the greatest intelligence in the universe?"

As Sine Anura had suggested, the weather slot was not ideal. One giant storm was twisting its way slowly westwards and a second was following a full short-period day behind. Since both were rotating in a clockwise direction, there was an eye of broken turbulence where the peripheral winds of the two great storms met head-on. It was in this 'eye' that the instruments reported blustery conditions with winds seldom exceeding a hundred miles an hour, and if it maintained its present course it would pass very close to the target area. The big question lay in the certainty of its course: it was an area of partial quiet formed between two regions of dynamic movement, and only a slight alteration in the intensity of either storm could cause the eye to veer sharply to the left or right, or even to disappear entirely. A descent at such a time was a pursuit fraught with uncertainties, but after watching the ever-increasing number of blips on the long-range radar, Ancor decided that they had no choice but to make the attempt. It was becoming reasonably certain that they would not get a second chance.

The first part of the descent was deceptively smooth. Though the wind speeds were enormous there was relatively little turbulence, and Cherry was able to nose the ship against the direction of the storm and ride a reasonably easy path down to less than a half mile above the ground. Here, however, resistance from the undulating ground slowed the violently circulating winds, setting a shear effect between the lower and upper layers, and when the *Shellback* entered this layer, trouble began. Suddenly the little ship was out of control, and for all its weight it was tossed and thrown like a leaf by the contemptuous forces which surrounded it. Its motors began firing in spasmodic bursts, desperately trying to correct its attitude, but the corrections always came too late to be effective.

Then as suddenly as the dramatic dance had begun, it was over, and miraculously they were in the mildly turbulent eye between the mammoth storms, and though the gusting was irregular, it seemed like perfect silence by comparison. Cherry's reckoning had been nearly exact, and the giant six-legged egg stood now no more than a mile away, looking strangely forlorn and lonely against the scoured terrain and the ominous blackness of the menacing cloud-race beyond.

Soon the ship was in position, and the grav-locks were applied, but they all knew, from the great depressions in the ground which had resulted from their former visit, that not even grav-locks could save the *Shellback* if the eye moved on and the storm-winds returned. This time Tez accompanied them to help Ancor with the receiver, and Sine came with extra ropes and auxiliary lamps. Ancor had planned the exploit well, and although the winds were uncomfortably strong they were seldom at great personal risk. Also the rain stayed away, so that they did not have to contend with the muddy spray, and their initial progress was swift and sure.

Using the rugged case of the receiver as a pedestal on which to stand whilst he reached into the open cavity, Ancor worked quickly. He and Tez had prepared all the leads in advance, and Sine stood by with the auxiliary lamp to supply the light. In point of fact the wiring operation took Ancor less than ten minutes, the prevailing conditions being so relatively calm that he was able to work completely without inerruption. Soon the receiver with its trailing leads was dragged to the nearest leg and there stoutly secured by straps and ropes. A quick check showed that the device was working properly, and they then sheeted it as best they could with heavy waterproof fabric against the probable return of the rain.

Then the calm eye in the weather moved on, and the sudden lash of a super-gale sent them all tumbling and sprawling. They had not, however, been deceived by the comparatively clement conditions in which they had worked, and they were all fully suited and with masks, and their safety harnesses were attached to the ship-line. Without these precautions one or more of them could easily have been lost, for the wind rose to such unprecedented levels that standing became a complete impossibility. With the wind came a violent sheeting of driven rain which instantly turned the surface into a dangerously slippery ooze. Ancor's planning had covered even this eventuality, and the ship-line had been paid out from the winch, which Carli, very very gently now used to drag back to the ship the three prone and desperate forms who bucked with each lash of the amazing squalls.

Tez was last inside, and it took the full power of the servos to close the hatch against the pressures of the gale. The space-lock looked like a mud-bath, and the slimed and panting figures who emerged from it resembled creatures newly arrived from the bottom of a grotesque area. Although the ship trembled with each thrust from the ever-increasing storm, the bed-rock to which they were secured by the grav-locks held promise of remaining firm at least for a limited period. Cherry, however, had a problem. The driving hurricane, already greater in force than on their first visit, was set in a direction such that if he released the grav-locks it might snatch the ship and hurl it bodily at the all too solid structure in front of it. Then as he miserably contemplated the difficulty of extricating the *Shellback* from this situation a new and even more worrying phenomenon arrived upon the scene.

In what appeared to be a vast explosion narrowly to their right, a violent fire-ball weighing so much that the ground beneath them rocked under the impact, ploughed a giant crater which extended nearly as far as the crouching ship and burst into streamers of incandescent metal which filled the whole area with plunging fire.

163

"What the hell was that?" asked Ancor weakly.

"It was a spacekeeper. Deliberate suicide dive. Came out of orbit at a speed which ensured that it got very hot but didn't entirely burn out in the atmosphere. And there's plenty more where that came from."

"Then get us out of here, Cherry."

"I daren't release the grav-locks with the storm in this direction. We'd be plastered all over that egg in seconds."

"Well if we sit here we're dead anyway. Those things can only be targeted during the first part of their flight. Once the frictional melt-down begins, the control surfaces will go and the mass has to continue on its set trajectory. So they could hit a sitting target with a fair degree of accuracy, but a moving target would be a more difficult proposition. Space-crash positions, everyone!"

"How do you want to play it, Maq?"

"Wind the thrusters up but keep the grav-locks engaged. Then slip the grav-locks at the last moment. We should go up like a cork out of a bottle."

"We'll tear the ship apart."

Another thunderbolt, this time to the left and approximately the same distance from them as the first, filled the whole atmosphere with flying fire.

"They're ranging us, Cherry. The next one will be a dead hit."

The quaking holo-illusionist at the controls had already figured the odds for himself and knew what the answers had to be. He brought the forward-thrusters and downjets up to full power with a single movement of his hands at the controls, and, pausing only to scan the signals which confirmed that space-crash emergency positions had been adopted, he waited until maximum thrust had been obtained, then switched off the grav-locks.

The stresses which both the ship and the crew encountered were probably the greatest to which either had been exposed in any previous exploit, and it was to the eternal credit of the *Shellback*'s designers that both the machinery and the men were able to survive it. The *Shellback*'s engines were many times more powerful than those normally employed to drive great exospheric liners around some of the shells, and they were incongruously powerful when installed on such a small ship as this. The ship literally exploded away from its compromised position, ignoring even the vast winds now gusting up to four hundred miles an hour, and threw itself up into the air in a fiery frenzy. Almost immediately another fireball burst down from the heavens and plunged into the precise space which the little ship had occupied literally only seconds before. Two of the giant spacekeepers, driven into a merging mass of incandescence by fast entry through the atmosphere, had struck together at the foot of the great egg, and had the *Shellback* remained it was an absolute certainty that the gallant little ship would have been destroyed completely.

Now they were jetting upwards and backwards, soon to adopt a curving random path as Cherry fought to regain control from the byplay of the great forces he had unleashed. The initial punch of the acceleration had nearly broken his neck but not quite, and he blessed the foresight of the designers of his safety seat who had exercised so much forethought on his behalf. Ancor, similarly cushioned, had been more fortunate in being able to force his position prone, whilst the others, snapped safely in the soft confines of space-crash cocoons, rode the experience relatively easily.

Soon the crushing pressures eased, and Cherry was throwing the *Shellback* confidently in long arcs, and the fireballs out of space continued to arrive. Ancor estimated that at least two hundred of the giant space vehicles which served and tended the orbiting luminaries must have been sacrificed in this deadly struggle. The possibility of the *Shellback*'s escape from the foot of the egg must have been precalculated, because the flaring tonnages of molten metal from the skies carpeted a broader area as they rose, although the length of time these successive missiles took to come from the exosphere was such that the decision as to where they were to fall must have been made whilst the little ship was still on the ground, and there could have been no further control of their positioning once the crucial meltdown had begun in the higher regions of the atmosphere. Because the *Shellback* was now moving, it could no longer be targeted, and if it was hit it would be purely by chance. However, a high degree of chance was assured by the staggering quantity of white-hot and molten masses of what had once been great space vehicles, which stormed down out of the torn and angry skies.

As soon as he had been able to free himself from the safety couch, Ancor had acquired the long-range radar, which showed the fantastic pattern of the bombardment as it developed up above. The great precision with which the fireballs had been falling despite the turbulent ground winds showed him that a complete set of information was being fed into the calculations for their suicide trajectories, and that a mammoth amount of computing power was being applied to the task. He wished he had the time to bring his own computer into play to anticipate the courses depicted on the screen and to guide the *Shellback* on a safe route in between. Instead, feeling rather like an ant trapped inside some deadly electronic game, he could only watch the indications of hurtling menace growing on the screen and attempt an estimation of when the ship was actually flying into danger. Cherry responded rapidly when Maq called for an urgent course correction, but even so, uncomfortably close encounters with plunging masses of molten debris were too frequent for comfort.

Even the tyrant, however, had only limited resources at his disposal, and finally the pace of the bombardment lessened and the remaining spacekeepers in station above them dwindled to only a few, with the occasional suicide dive remaining as scarcely more than a token gesture and being easily avoided by the watchful Ancor. Finally the *Shellback* climbed above the driving winds and circled back over the egg-shaped executive centre. Using the scanner because the cloud cover would not permit him to use the telescope for direct visual observation, Ancor examined the area carefully. The targeting of the plunging ships had been so precisely controlled that nothing had fallen on the egg itself, although there was a close pattern of metal-spattered craters all around it.

Ancor's great fear was that some of the streams of molten metal flung out when the fireballs struck might have damaged the receiver or the vulnerable connections leading to the coupling beneath the belly of the great structure. Such information as they could gain from their high altitude, however, was insufficient to enable him to determine whether the receiver was damaged or not. Nor, since the receiver had not been fitted with a repeater, was it possible to determine electronically whether the device was still in operation.

Knowing that he had no alternative but to continue with the operation anyway, Ancor began to transmit the information which Zeus had loaded into the ship's computer memory banks, and hoped against hope that the tactic would be effective. Although its power modules were regarded as being inexhaustible, most of the armaments and other supplies in the *Shellback* were running critically low, and if they were ever to return to their base at Zapoketa on Saturn shell and ultimately to their homes on Mars shell, they would soon have to start that journey, perhaps never knowing whether their mission had been a success or not.

CHAPTER TWENTY-NINE

Massacre

"WHERE TO NOW?" asked Cherry, after the transmission was finished.

Ancor was examining his stores' lists dubiously.

"I'd promised Kyns Ala we would try and repeat at another spoke-terminal what we had already done at his, but the logistics of the operation don't look so good. So I think we'll merely visit him and see if he needs any assistance. After that, we head for home."

"And the tyrant?"

"I don't know what was in that message packet Zeus got us to deliver to the egg—nor do I know if it even got there. It's also inconceivable to me that any package of electronic signals delivered to a single point could reverse what's been taking place here. But there's nothing else we can do. Even with our topmode speed approaching half a million miles an hour in free space, it would take us four years non-stop flight just to circumnavigate the Neptune shell once. It would take a lifetime or better to attempt to visit every executive centre on the shell."

Cherry sucked his lip. "I'll take us back to the spoke-terminal. Do you reckon those up there will give us any trouble?" He was nodding to where the few remaining spacekeepers were still circling in high station.

"They're big enough not to be able to take us unawares, and once we reach the high exosphere we can outrun them if we choose. But the whole scene has gone strangely quiet, and I'm wondering if Zeus hasn't already applied some sort of countermand order."

"It hasn't had time yet," objected Cherry. "You said eight hours was the absolute minimum."

"That's true, but I wonder if the signals we fed to the egg

aren't already having some effect. There would be one way to find out, and that would be to get up there among those 'keepers and see how they react."

Cherry considered the prospect nervously. "I doubt it's worth taking the risk, Maq. As far as I'm concerned, the only safe spacekeeper is one so far out in space that it won't even register on the screens."

In point of fact the giant space vessels paid no attention at all to the little craft as it soared towards the exosphere, and sixteen hours later the *Shellback* was nearing the great, golden shaft of the spoke-freight system. Their entire flight had been uneventful, but even from a height it was possible to see that disaster had struck at the terminal. The Exis tube of the spoke itself was immune to any ordinary physical forces, but the terminal buildings had been crushed or torn apart by something unimaginably strong, and even the massive spiral railway of the insertion and withdrawal loops had been twisted and mangled and now lay uncomfortably exposed to the great, brooding sky.

They circled low, trying to ascertain the extent of the damage and its probable cause. The wreckage showed none of the characteristics of destruction by an explosion, and Ancor's best estimate was that one of Zeus' great terraforming engines, used during the construction of a shell to raise mountains and dig seas, had been called in and set to produce this particular piece of mischief. He breathed a sigh of relief: there was no way the emigrant army could have failed to see or hear it coming, and though it had destroyed their initial refuge it was unlikely to have taken many lives. Of the machine itself they saw no sign, but at its low speed it could not have travelled very far away.

Initially they found no signs of life, but as they were making a landing nearby three figures rushed from a shelter in the wreckage and ran towards them.

"What's the situation here?" asked Ancor as they approached.

"Terrifying," was the glum assurance. "We made a camp in the terminal and in the galleries below. Kyns Ala thought to make it a fortress from which we could expand slowly, and three more shuttles arrived, each with a hundred and fifty emigrants to help us. The red-hats came in force with their stun-guns, but we beat them off and captured a number of their hover-vehicles. Then they set their robots on us, and we were powerless. They literally tore us apart, and it was the most filthy massacre I've ever seen."

"Many killed?"

"About half of us. I suppose better than three hundred. The rest of us retreated to the galleries and tried to barricade the entrance. The robots took the stuff away as fast as we could pile it there, and occasionally one broke through and smashed everyone in sight, but at least we slowed them down. But it was all a frightful nightmare, and we were running short of food and water. Then some sort of machine arrived which smashed the whole place down, and I think there are still a lot of them trapped in the gallery.''

''Some possibly still alive?'' asked Ancor sharply.

''I think so. But the entrance is buried under tons of wreckage.''

''Come and show me.'' Ancor invited the speaker into the ship and hurriedly directed Cherry to hover over the spot where the ramp leading to the underground installation had been located. Sure enough the massive concrete roof, its supports and beams undercut, had sealed off the area entirely, and he dropped down on to the fractured blocks to see for himself if anything could be done. Moving a substantial span of the fallen roof would have been an impossibility even with the thrust power available to the *Shellback*, but there was one large concrete beam in a critical position which he thought they could tackle and which might leave a sufficient gap through which a rescue might be attempted. With their very last space-alloy cable and a great deal of concerned sweating they finally managed to secure the beam to the *Shellback*'s lifting hooks, and the great struggle began.

Initially the task proved too much even for the ship's powerful engines, because large areas of the fractured roof were still attached by metal reinforcing straps. Ancor and Tez picked away at these with heavy-duty lasers, and soon the beam came free and was swung deftly sideways away from the location of the ramp. A swift return to hitch up some other debris, during which operation Ancor stayed down on the broken roof to give directions, and a cavity leading down to the underground corridor was revealed. Ancor waved Cherry and the ship away and picked his way carefully through the debris to where he could actually see the littered slope of the ramp leading down into the darkness. He dropped through to see what further impediments there were to the escape of those trapped below. The immediate sound of movements in the gloom was a reassuring sign that there was life to be found and that with the beam now removed there were growing hopes of recovery.

He passed on downwards, finding the whole ramp filled with miscellanea which he presumed had been used as part of the barricade. More sickeningly, the piles of mute and mangled bodies were ample evidence of the diabolical effectiveness of the robots against unarmed men. Then he came to a high jam of pieces and fractured debris, some of which he was able to lift by himself and gradually to clear away. The sounds told him hopefully of a similar operation being carried out on the other side of the pile, and he renewed his efforts until finally a narrow opening came clear.

In the dimness a hand came through, and he went to grasp it, hoping at least to offer reassurance. Then he realised his mistake. He did not need a light to know that the steely grip around his right wrist was that of a robot . . .

CHAPTER THIRTY

Long Live The King

HIS LEFT HAND came up automatically with a handgun loaded with s.h.e. pellets, but he dared not fire. At such close range the fragmentation, whether he stopped the robot or not, would be suicidally fatal to himself. Indeed, the gun's best application, he thought wryly to himself, would be to turn it against his own head: a quick, clean death rather than suffer having his limbs torn off by the mechanical atrocity which held him.

However, a curious and unexpected thing occurred. After a few convulsive moments which nearly broke his wrist, the mechanical hand released him and withdrew. Amazed at this piece of luck, Ancor backed up the littered ramp until he had achieved a position where he could safely use the gun on the monster when it finally broke through. Shortly the remainder of the barricade disintegrated, kicked apart from the other side, and Maq strained his eyes trying to peer into the darkness ready to shoot the instant he could see the robot's form. The emerging shape which he finally detected, however, was not quite what he had expected. Certainly it was a robot, but cradled carefully in its arms was the prostrate figure of a man.

Ancor withheld his fire, not knowing if the figure being carried was dead or still alive. As the pair advanced up the ramp to where the cleared portion of the roof admitted daylight, he could see that the man was an emigrant and not a red-hat, and from an occasional involuntary groan it was obvious that he was injured but not dead. The care with which the robot picked its way through the debris, deliberately avoiding any shocks to the one in its arms, struck a curious note in Ancor's mind, and whilst holding the weapon steady, he stepped aside to let the man and the machine go safely past. Higher up the ramp the robot paused to scan for a route out from the blocked head of the ramp. It was not an easy prospect, but it deliberately kicked a block of fractured concrete weighing probably half a ton to a position where it could use it as a step, and with infinite care not to stress or damage its burden, it climbed up on to a section of the fallen roof and laid its charge delicately to rest. Then it turned and came back.

On the ramp it encountered Ancor, continued on a course which was obviously one of avoidance, and went on back down to the corridor beneath. Ancor had been intending to destroy it, but something about the machine's attitude made him decide to follow it instead. This robot had carried an injured man out from under ground, and had twice passed Ancor without more than a cursory glance. This was typical of more normal domestic robot activity, shorn of all the savage urge to destruction which the red-hats had been able to impart to them. So either all the red-hats in the district were dead and their influence had gone. Or . . . or else the tyrant, the link between the men and the machines, was deposed . . .

Swiftly Ancor flung himself down the slope in the wake of the descending robot. The barricade had been broken when the machine had come through, but the robot now paused and was intent on clearing a wider gap. Ancor stopped alongside and began to help, and soon they were working co-operatively and a way through was cleared. In the corridor a couple of dim emergency lights were operating, and for this low light level Ancor was glad because it stopped him from being able to see in too much detail the results of the recent carnage which had taken place. Additionally, the weight of the terraforming machine which had destroyed the terminal had distorted much of the corridor's roof, and massive concrete segments now hung precariously low and dangerous. It was in trying to estimate why some of these had not fallen completely that Ancor received further confirmation that the hand of the tyrant was removed. Braced like pit-props in the darkness stood half a dozen robots with the crushing roof-weight suspended entirely on their bending backs. They were sacrificing themselves to let the trapped humans escape.

"Is anyone still there?" Ancor called through the low passage beneath the fallen ceiling. "You'd best come out fast if you can, because the roof won't hold."

"Damn the roof! At least the robots can't get us and tear our arms off." The voice through the tunnel sounded sick and exhausted.

"The robots will help you, not attack you now."

"Are you crazy? They're killers."

"Not any more."

172

"Who says so?"

"It is I, Maq Ancor. We have returned with the *Shellback*."

There was the sound of movement in the tunnel and finally about thirty emigrants, wearied and dirty and with faces which fully reflected their recent experiences, came through, some half carrying, half dragging injured comrades.

"Any more left through there?" asked Ancor.

"None it would help to bring out. Poor devils!" The speaker's eyes were fixed with frightened fascination on the dark robot who stood at Ancor's side. "How the hell did you manage to tame this bloody tin atrocity?"

"They weren't made as killers, they were made as domestic aids. But the tyrant gained control of them, just as he gained control of the red-hats. Now all the signs are that the tyrant is finished."

"Dead?"

"Death doesn't apply to entities like that." Ancor shook his head and declined to discuss the matter further. With an amazing precision the robot at his side picked up one of the injured men, cradled him carefully in his arms, and began to bear him along the corridor towards the ramp. As it turned, Ancor was able to see that the man being carried was Kyns Ala, who would now be a permanent cripple and for whom the dream of empire had gone remarkably sour.

Slowly the rescuers and rescued were brought together out on the plain clear of the ruined terminal. In all, less than two hundred of them remained. Somehow, Cherry had managed to locate some of the shuttle vehicles and used the *Shellback* to drag them out of the ruins to places where they would have to serve as shelter and hospital until the group could find or build something better.

A foraging party was organised to search the area where the stores had been located in the terminal, and this brought back a small but useful amount of food, and a supply of water was also found. The most encouraging prospect for the future, however, was the continuing arrival of new robots. These, without any instruction, had set themselves to work tidying the wreckage and unceremoniously burying the uncovered dead. Others had appeared more distantly and seemed to be marking-out and preparing fields for planting. Suddenly, survival was a possibility.

Then there was panic as a dozen red-hats with their hover-vehicles came into view. The emigrants feared another attack, and the *Shellback* took to the air to cover the oncoming caravan. Their fears were needless, however. The red-hats brought medical supplies and food and seeds and were concerned that the emigrant colony should survive. By careful questioning Ancor established that they were no longer being controlled by ESB transmissions, although the point was difficult to establish because they had seldom been consciously aware of external interference with their thoughts. As far as they were concerned, they were reacting to this emergency as they would have reacted to any other, and this showed just how subtle the hand of the tyrant had been. This time they were being motivated by their own instincts, and the only difference they had noticed was that they tended to disagree more frequently instead of acting with their accustomed unison.

Finally came the time when the *Shellback* had to leave. The emigrant colony would undoubtedly have difficulties getting established, but none that would be greatly eased by the continued presence of an armed ship. Cherry and Tez had made an aerial survey of the surrounding area and produced a composite map showing the nature of the terrain, location of rivers, etc., which would be useful to the colony when it started to expand, as expand it must. If it followed the normal Solarian pattern of doubling in population every thirty years, the two hundred who now remained could fill even the mighty Neptune shell in around seventy generations. More seriously, if the red-hats were now free to follow their own instincts, the five thousand million million of them who already existed could saturate the shell with human kind in a mere thirteen generations.

As the *Shellback* lifted, Ancor's face was stern. Under the yoke of the tyrant, the population of the Neptune shell had been stable, and their way of life could have been maintained through all eternity. Now that the tyrant no longer ruled, a mere four hundred years would elapse before the inhabitants of these vastest of all lands in Solaria would again be crying out for living space. What if the tyrant had been right—that it made more sense to find a way to control the remorseless growth of population rather than attempt continually to create extra room for a race growing nearly exponentially? Suddenly Ancor was unsure. There were clear indications that the Solarian universe could not continue to expand out towards infinity. Physics alone forbade that many more shells could be added before the end was reached.

Sine Anura found Ancor sitting in front of the computer. The depth of his concentration was such that it almost amounted to a coma. A glance at the screen told her what it was which occupied his mind. Written upon it was a list of all the known great concentric shells of the Solarian universe: Mercury, Venus, Earth, Mars, Aster, Jupiter, Boxa, Saturn, Uranus and Neptune, tabulated with their estimated populations. At the bottom was an approximate total which Ancor had translated out of the scientific notation and read: SIXTY MILLION MILLION MILLION MILLION SOULS. He had obviously started to perform some extra calculations on the sum and had then been overcome by the sheer enormity of the problem.

After a while he became aware of her, and looked up, a slightly rueful smile upon his face.

"You can't do it, Maq," she said. "No man can take the worries of Solaria on his own shoulders."

"Perhaps because we've been right through Solaria we can see it more clearly than most, Sine. But you can spell it out easily. Shuffle populations between the shells any way you want, but the answer always comes out the same: the Solarian universe is nearly full of people. Thirty years from now it will be twice as full, and in a further thirty years it will be twice as full again. So what is going to give? Will all humanity choke itself to death? Or is there somewhere out there past the shell of Pluto where men can continue to live?"

"We can't answer that, Maq. Nobody's ever been out that far and returned to tell what they saw."

"Then we shall go, Sine. One day we'll take the *Shellback* right out to the edge of the universe itself."

"That's a long haul, Maq."

"Very long. But out there are regions beyond the limits of our imagination. Our there are things which even Zeus can't tame. If mankind has a future, it starts at that final edge. That's what I've got to see, Sine. I need to *know* what's there."

She ran her fingers through his hair caressingly. "We both need to know, Maq. And where you go, I go. After all, as a team we didn't do so bad against the tyrant."

"With a little help from our friend Zeus, of course. I've been trying to figure out exactly how that trick was worked. How, by re-programming one executive centre Zeus appears to have regained control of the whole. I think the answer must be that we didn't kill the tyrant, we usurped him. The tyrant was a conspiracy between a number of similar executive centres spread right around the shell. That program simply made one of them immensely more powerful than the rest. And while that one remains loyal to Zeus the rest are powerless to do other than conform. It's the good old human principle of government by wielding the big stick. All we've done is to replace the tyrant with a powerful king."

"Long live the king!" said Sine Anura.

Somewhere far ahead of them, as yet an unseen detail against the mighty brow of the horizon, was a thousand-mile high 'volcano' marking the cageworld aperture which would be the first leg of their long route home. That such a mighty structure would shrink to insignificance was a true measure of the size of the mighty shell of Neptune, and the others eagerly searched the great sweep of the terrain, each trying to be the first to point it out. Ancor's eyes, however, were turned in the opposite direction. He was looking outwards through Hades-space to where theory told him lay the even greater shell of Pluto. And beyond Pluto, what . . . ? An end or a new beginning?

Though his eyes could tell him nothing, his gaze was unwavering and his thoughts were spanning a thousand million miles to the edge of the Solarian universe. One day soon he knew that just thinking about it was not going to be enough. One day he was going there to see . . .